MY WORK IS NOT YET DONE

Three Tales of Corporate Horror

Thomas Ligotti

Published by Virgin Books 2009

2 4 6 8 10 9 7 5 3 1

First published in hardback in the USA by Mythos Books 2002

Copyright © Thomas Ligotti 2002

Thomas Ligotti has asserted his right under the Copyright, Designs and Patents
Act 1988 to be identified as the author of this work.

'I Have a Special Plan for This World' and 'The Nightmare Network' previously
appeared in *Horror Garage* and *Darkside: Horror for the Next Millennium*,
respectively.

First published in Great Britain in 2009 by
Virgin Books
Random House, 20 Vauxhall Bridge Road,
London SW1V 2SA

www.virginbooks.com
www.rbooks.co.uk

Addresses for companies within The Random House Group Limited can be
found at: www.randomhouse.co.uk/offices.htm

The Random House Group Limited Reg. No. 954009

A CIP catalogue record for this book is available from the British Library

ISBN 9780753516881

The Random House Group Limited supports The Forest Stewardship Council
[FSC], the leading international forest certification organisation. All our titles
that are printed on Greenpeace approved FSC certified paper carry the FSC logo.
Our paper procurement policy can be found at
www.rbooks.co.uk/environment

Typeset by TW Typesetting, Plymouth, Devon

Printed in the UK by CPI Bookmarque, Croydon, CR0 4TD

CONTENTS

MY WORK IS NOT YET DONE

Part I

1

I had always been afraid. However, as self-serving as this may sound, I never believed this to be a cause for shame or regret, even though an intolerable suffering may ensue from such a trait. It seemed to me that the finest people, as people go, cannot help but betray a fair portion of fear and insecurity, even full-blown panic. On the other hand, someone must have a considerable dose of the swine in their make-up to get through even a single day unafflicted by trepidations of one sort or another, not to mention those who go out of their way to court dangerous encounters, fearlessly calling attention to themselves, figuratively waving their arms and declaring to everyone within range, 'Hey, look at me. I'm up here. See what I can do. I'm the one you have to knock down. I'm the one.'

Of course there is a measure of beast's blood in anyone who aspires to maintain a place in the world, anyone who lacks that ultimate decency to remove themselves from the herd either by violence to themselves or total capitulation to their dread. It's simply a matter of degree.

At the company where I had been a longtime employee, the purest breed of swine was represented by the seven persons with whom I met in a conference room according to a weekly schedule. I had risen, somewhat reluctantly but with a definite touch of swinishness, to the position of a supervisor in my division of a company in which there were countless other divisions. This made it necessary to attend these meetings along with six others of my kind and a seventh who was our superior by virtue of his having outswined the rest of us.

During a meeting of my own staff, someone whose mind was not fixated, as was mine, on the swine analogy, referred to these persons with whom I met, according to a weekly schedule, as The Seven Dwarfs.

'So what does that make me, Dave – Snow White?'

'No, Frank,' interjected Lisa, 'that would make you Prince, uh, what's-his-name.'

'Charming,' said Lois.

'Pardon me?' replied Lisa.

'Prince Charming. Didn't you at least see the movie?'

This remark caused a hurt look to cross Lisa's face. It was a good one, very realistic.

'Hey, I was just kidding,' said Lois, who wasn't easily taken in by false or exaggerated phenomena.

Lisa perked up again on cue and continued. 'That's right, Prince Charming.'

'Well, thanks for saying that, Lisa,' I said. But I wasn't quick enough to head off Christine.

'We usually talk nice about Frank behind his back. But it's okay, you've only been here a week.'

'I'm sorry if it sounded like I was trying to score points or something,' said Lisa, actually sounding quite sincere this time. 'The department where I used to work –'

'You're not there any more,' I said. 'You're here. And everyone here used to work somewhere else in the company.'

'Except you, Frank,' said Elias. 'You've been in this department forever.'

'True enough,' I replied.

* * *

After the meeting with my staff ended I proceeded immediately to the other meeting, where I intended to play the swine in a way I had never tried before. I had a new idea to present to my colleagues, which of course would involve a considerable amount of arm-waving and look-at-me behavior. It had been some time since I had reaccredited myself with my peers, and I was beginning to suffer from an uncomfortable sense that my standing with these persons was in question.

This is the paradox of always being afraid: while the pangs of apprehension and self-consciousness may allow you to imagine yourself as a being created of finer materials than most, a certain level of such agony necessarily drives you to grovel for the reassurances and approval of swine, or dwarfs if you like, who function as conductors of a fear from which they themselves do not appear to suffer. And how well they're able to control this fear, turning it in your direction at will and causing its dreadful current to flow just long enough to send you running to them so that you may be allowed to make a case for your own swinehood, hoping to prove that you are an even bigger swine, or a smaller dwarf, than they. This is the only thing that can bring some relief from that most pernicious form of being afraid – the anxiety provoked by other people and what they may do to you, either collectively or as individual agents.

Tragically, the same fear that allows you to believe yourself a better specimen of the human species than those around you can only be tolerated for so long. Anything beyond that point, any excess of anxiety, and you begin to imagine yourself closeted in a little room somewhere under heavy sedation or to consider an act of slaughter against yourself (or perhaps against others). Thus I was aching with hopes for my new idea, my special plan to increase the prosperity of the company – that institutional manifestation of the swine. I longed for it to receive the snuffling high-sign of my fellow wallowers in filth, the low-voiced sanction (or so I hoped) of the seven *other* dwarfs. Needless to say, I was terror-stricken.

2

As usual I was the first to arrive in the conference room where I met with the six other supervisors in the division and with Richard, our manager. This room was located outside the modernized office space wherein most of the company carried out its activities and was a place that still exhibited, unharmed by refurbishing, the pre-Depression style of the building in which the company occupied several floors. I was never sure what purpose the room was originally intended to serve, but it was disproportionately large and lofty for the small talk of business that echoed within its realm. Furthermore, it was quite dimly lighted by the rows of ornately sconced fixtures that jutted out at intervals from faded and intricate wallpaper which had peeled away in spots. One could barely see the crumbled moldings interposed between the upper edges of the walls and the shadowy ceiling.

The table at which I and the others met seemed to have been imported from the banquet hall of an earlier century, while the enormous leather chairs in which our bodies truly appeared of dwarfish size had become brittle over the years and creaked like old floorboards whenever we shifted within them. There was a row of tall paned windows along one of the walls, each of them still valanced but without curtains. I liked to look out of these windows because they offered a view of the river as well as a fine panorama of several other old office buildings.

However, on that particular morning a heavy spring fog had lingered long enough to obstruct any view of the river and had turned the other buildings in the downtown area into specters of themselves, only the nearest of which could be seen to cast their illumination through the fog like strange lighthouses. And I was grateful to the aging monuments of the city for providing me, by no means for the first time, with a calming perspective that only a vision of degeneration and decline can bestow.

Soon enough, though, the others arrived and took their places, setting down upon the already scarred finish of the table their outsized mugs of coffee or towering containers of bottled water. I never failed to wonder how they were able to consume such incredible quantities of coffee, water, fruit juice, and what have you during these meetings, which always went on for at least an hour. I myself made a point of *not* taking in unaccustomed amounts of liquid prior to these weekly convocations, just so that I might avoid the necessity of disrupting the proceedings by bursting out of the room in search of the nearest lavatory.

But none of the others appeared to have the least problem in this area, however closely I scrutinized them for tell-tale signs of stress. Least of all did Richard seem bothered by such bodily strain, since he always showed up with not only the largest container of coffee but also a huge thermos from which he would at least twice refill his great barrel of a cup on which was emblazoned the company logo. Just watching them gulp mouthful after mouthful of their various liquids sometimes brought fantasies of a gleaming row of urinals to my mind. Perhaps they all wore special undergarments, I once considered, and freely relieved themselves as we spoke about budgets and headcounts, speed to market and out-sourcing.

All of which is simply to say that my co-functionaries within the division, along with Richard, were a complete mystery to me on every level. They seemed to me as fantastic beings who well deserved the fairy-tale designation of The Seven Dwarfs, even though there was a more mundane and obvious reason for calling them such. This reason, I should point out, did not derive from any shared qualities between Dopey, Grumpy, Sleepy, and the rest of that cute and hard-working crew, and the seven persons, not including myself, now seated at that nicely decrepit table.

My fellow supervisors, plus Richard, were neither con-spicuously cute (with one exception) nor hard-working. But their names were, no kidding, Barry, Harry, Perry, Mary, Kerrie, Sherry, and, of course, Richard, whom I had heard referred to as 'The Doctor', although the origin of this nickname, which was a matter of both credible anecdote and curious imaginings, in no way linked him with the dwarfish Doc of the fairy tale.

Richard finally cleared his throat with a forced, rattling sound that was his way of bringing the meeting to order. Everyone stopped chatting and turned toward the head of the table, where sat the only one of us whose chair didn't appear too big for his body. But Richard's stature was more than that of someone who purchased his suits at clothes stores catering to large-bodied men. His physical conformation, straight and solid from head to toe, was imposingly athletic, the anatomy of an erstwhile ball-player of some kind who had kept his shape into middle age. In all probability Richard had garnered his share of shining trophies for the glory of Self and School. He wouldn't be the first member of middle- to upper-level corporate management with a background in the world of sport, with all the playing-field metaphors they borrowed from that milieu, chief among them being all that puke-inducing nonsense about teams (the characterization of someone as a 'team player' was at the top of my line-up of emetic expressions of this sort).

'All right, then, let's get started,' barked Richard as he stared down at a page on the table that listed the agenda items for that week's meeting. 'Looks like you're first up, Domino. Something to do with New Product.'

For the record: my last name is not Domino; it's Dominio, with two 'i's.

For the record: I had attempted to correct Richard both publicly and privately regarding the accurate form of my surname.

For the record: I could never be absolutely sure that it wasn't pure indifference rather than a taste for malicious mockery that accounted for his persistently calling me Domino, although this sly mangling of my name never failed to draw a few muted snickers from the others, and Richard could not have been oblivious to that.

Like a dealer at a poker game, I quickly passed around to my colleagues the two-page proposal I had distilled from a much longer document. This hand-out was composed with wide margins and a large font for speedy absorption into the systems of busy middle-management types. I tried not to look around the table as they all glanced it over, turning from page one to page two almost simultaneously. When Richard was finished he laid the document on the table before him and gazed upon it as if he were looking at a bowl of cereal in which he thought he might have spotted something unsavory . . . or possibly peering into a riverbed in which he glimpsed a shiny nugget in the shallows of clear water.

'Forgive me, Frank,' said Richard, 'but I'm not sure I understand what this is supposed to be?'

I sat up as high as I could in my giant's chair.

'At the last meeting you said that New Product was putting out one of their rare calls for suggestions for, well, new product ideas. This is a proposal for a new product, possibly an entire line of new product.'

'That much I comprehend, thank you. It's just, um, this is a little far afield from what I think anyone had in mind.'

'I realize how it might seem that way. This is why I thought I would bring it up initially at this meeting. I'd consider whatever feedback anyone might have to be of value before I submitted my proposal in full.'

'There's more to this?' asked Richard.

'Quite a bit, yes,' I said.

'Hmm. That's really something. I can only wonder where you found the time, given that the rest of us have been frantically trying to dig our way out of one landslide or another that's threatening to bury us around here.'

'I did almost all of it on my own time, if that's your concern,' I said.

'My only concern,' replied Richard as he slowly looked around the table at the other supervisors, 'my primary concern, I should say, is that the New Product idea you're proposing doesn't look like the sort of thing we do around here. I mean, I'm all for being risky and innovative and all that, but this is . . . hoo boy.'

'But we *could* do it,' I argued. 'We have the people, the know-how, all the processes in place already.'

'True enough,' admitted Richard. 'But I don't know. Does anyone else have any thoughts about this?'

'It *is* different,' said Perry.

'Definitely different,' said Harry.

'I'm not sure we do in fact have the staff needed to take on something like this,' said Mary.

'I've got fewer people taking on more projects all the time,' said Kerrie.

'*Systemically*,' Barry began, instantly losing the attention of his auditors. At one juncture in his jargon-polluted soliloquy of a business analyst he used the words 'data vamping,' which I believe was a neologism of his own devising. Ultimately, of course, he sided with Richard, concluding that my idea, which Barry explained had built into it at least two, perhaps two *and a half* 'facets', was not 'leverage focused', nor was it 'customerly', in Barry's opinion.

Sherry was at a characteristic loss to add anything to the litany of negation already recited by the others, although she did manage to come up with 'faster, better, cheaper', which on this occasion might be construed to mean that my proposal was not quite in line with this triple-headed ideal.

By this point I was writhing within the creaking depths of my chair, shaking my head in a slight palsy of horror and forming phrases in my mind that refused to come together into coherent sentences. Then, for a brief moment, the words congealed.

'I know that the company has traditionally produced only that which looks like what it has previously produced – in other words, recycled impersonations of what we've been doing for the past two decades.'

'It's called leveraging, Frank. It's what we do, and it's still managing a good margin.'

'But for how much longer?'

'Look,' said Richard, 'I enjoy brainstorming new ideas as much as the next guy. It's just that, by bringing this to me, to all of us, it's like asking for a sanction of some kind. And that's asking a lot. How about if you hold off on this a while. Give us all some time to think this over and revisit the whole thing at a later date. What do you say?'

'Sure,' I said, positive that this matter would never arise again.

'Fine,' said Richard. 'Now let's move on to the next item on the agenda.'

And for the rest of the meeting I tried not to betray my inner turmoil. Moreover, I couldn't keep my mind from its obsession with a new terror: the sense that I had been the victim of an ambush – that no scheme that I might have advanced before that particular gathering stood a chance, that whatever plan I had brought to that meeting and laid upon that time-ravaged table would have died there.

Outside the windows of that antiquated room the fog was slowly fading away, revealing once again a view of the river and a cityscape in which my mind moved among scenes of calming decay.

3

Fear, when blended with failure, distills into a deadly brew. I had been so caught up in what I thought was the brilliance of my new idea, my special plan, that I never seriously pondered the consequences of it being rejected out of hand by the very persons I most wanted to accept it. This was a miscalculation of vast proportions, no question about it. For the rest of that morning, as I sat in my supervisor's cubicle, I could do nothing but inwardly reproach myself for being a creature of deranged judgment . . . and not even that: I was no more than a primitive organism with no faculty of judgment whatever, a slick of slime mold posing as a human being. 'You're making too much of this,' said one of those secondary selves that are implanted inside every one of us and that come to attention on these occasions, spitting forth idiotic clichés like a mad schoolmaster from a worn-out textbook of conventional wisdom. 'In the grand scheme of things,' the voice continued before I grabbed it with both hands and wrung its neck, spitting out my words of contempt through gritted teeth –

A: There is no grand scheme of things.

B: If there were a grand scheme of things, the fact – the *fact* – that we are not equipped to perceive it, either by natural or supernatural means, is a nightmarish obscenity.

C: The very notion of a grand scheme of things is a nightmarish obscenity.

When Galileo brought his findings before the board of directors at Vatican Inc., he was at least armed with facts that reasonably supported his botched attempt to deal with those who endorsed the obscene notion of a grand scheme of things. He could *know* that he was right, even though he was also an utter fool for sharing what he knew with the wrong people.

I couldn't know anything about the worth of my idea, my plan; its value resided exclusively in the estimation of the people around me, especially Richard. It didn't matter – not even to me – whether or not it would prove to be a source of profit to the company, in the unlikely event that the greater powers of that commercial entity ever acted on my plans. Most initiatives did not amount to much. The important thing was to demonstrate that my four cloven feet were skittering swinishly in the same direction as those of everyone else. The debacle that took place at the meeting that foggy morning merely served to give away what I most wanted to hide: that I was moving in an entirely different direction from the rest of them.

My only recourse now was to follow Galileo's example and recant my ridiculous idea, my special plan. Why my mind had brought forth such a scheme had begun to confound even me. I knew what I was supposed to say and do in my position at the company, and those duties did not involve any kind of innovation or brilliance whatever. From that moment I forswore such things as abominations and vowed never again to conceive a new thought or scheme or plan unless bidden to do so, a task I knew would never be inflicted on me. I would say and do only that which I was supposed to say and do. That was all. That and only that.

But as my mind was still spinning in this groove of histrionic vows and disavowals, swearings and swearings off, the hulking shape of Richard appeared at the entrance to my cubicle.

'Got a minute?' he asked.

'Sure,' I said as he was already stepping into my workspace and making himself at home. In his fist was a copy of the two-page hand-out delineating the proposal I had proffered earlier that morning.

'Okay, here's how it is. Number one – I'm not saying that I'm going to make myself a signatory to any of this, or that I endorse it in any way,' he said, lightly shaking at me the two-page hand-out he was holding. 'Number two – I don't want you to think that I'm a complete villain and that my function around here is to squash your spirit every chance I get. Therefore, I've decided to pass this along to New Product – no special delivery, no marching bands or fanfare, just push it into their mailbox and see what they make of it. Cut this down to a single page, a half-page would be even better, and send it to me. I'll forward it to the NP crew along with some other communiqués I have for them. Can you live with that?'

'Yes, I can. Thanks very much.'

I sounded casual enough, or so I believed, but at that moment I could not help feeling a curative relief streaming through my system. I had been saved. And despite all the bitter renunciations that had echoed over and over only moments before in the darkness inside me, I had now become swollen with gratitude. Was this how Richard had acquired his rumored nickname? Thank you, Doc!

'Maybe we can even fit in your product idea for further discussion at next week's meeting,' continued Richard. 'How's that sound?'

'Sounds fine.'

'All right, then,' said Richard, turning to exit my cubicle. But he caught himself in mid-turn and doubled back. 'Uh, Frank,' he said in what sounded to me a lowered tone of voice.

'Yes?'

'Along with the memo for New Product, perhaps you should forward to me the rest of the work you've done on this,' Richard said, once again rattling the two-page hand-out in the air.

'As I said at the meeting, I worked on this almost entirely at home. And that's where it is right now. Some of it's still in hand-written form. I'll clean it all up and send it to you as soon as I can, if that's okay.' I hadn't missed a beat in my response to Richard's request, and yet for an unmeasurable splinter of a moment I saw him turn to stone before my eyes and fix a granite gaze upon me.

'Of course,' he said.

After Richard walked off I waited until I thought it was safe, and then I collapsed my upper body across the counter of my cubicle. *He knew*, I thought. He knew I was lying to him. I had the entire proposal on a disk and printed out in polished form as a stack of fiftysome pages in the lower drawer of my desk. I opened the drawer to check that its contents were actually still there. They were, even though for some delirious reason I thought they might not be. I touched the disk and flipped through the pages several times. They were still there. I closed the desk drawer. Then I opened it again and repeated my inspection a few more times before finally locking the drawer and placing the key inside my wallet.

What I still could not understand was the reason for my deception. It had been committed as an act of pure instinct, without any rational basis. It couldn't have been that I was afraid that Richard was going to steal my proposal and arrange to take credit for it himself, I thought. Others had done that to me over the years, and I was never the least put out by their betrayal. I wasn't looking to move any higher in the company than my present position, so why should I care about making time with anyone but my immediate superior?

I wanted to stay where I was, I wanted to keep my working life securely in the status quo, and I wanted to be left alone. This had been the motive for all my actions in my job. This was why employees of a similar disposition transferred to my department whenever there was an opening. We were a troupe of contented parasites, self-made failures, and complacent losers. What lives we had were carried on entirely outside the psychic perimeter of the company. We did our jobs and did them as well as or better than anyone else in that organization. And then we went home and spent time with our families or worked in our gardens or painted pictures or simply did nothing at all. Whatever we sought to attain in this precarious and – in all candor – wretched world, we looked for *outside the company*.

Of course I could always send my full proposal the very next day, and Richard could then do with it what he wished. In that sense I had done myself no special harm. But he would still know that I had lied to him, and I had no idea what that might mean.

4

Three days passed. On each of those days immediately upon waking from my senseless or scary dreams, I said to myself, 'Today I'm going to send Richard the document of my plan.' At the end of each day, having sent nothing to Richard, I said to myself, 'Tomorrow, without fail, I'm going to send Richard the document of my plan.'

So why was I stalling in this matter? Why was I setting out on a course that was clearly one of self-destruction, compounding my existing offense of having lied to Richard with that of blatant contempt for his instructions to send him the complete document of my plan? A provisional answer to this question came to me slowly over the course of those three days. And it had begun with that weekly meeting at which I felt myself to be the victim of ambush by all of them, not only Richard. His was simply the biggest and most hideous head of the monster: six others also emanated from the body of the beast, circling on long, snaky necks about the expansive and twisted face at the center of the thing, with its bloodshot eyes and killing breath (Richard did in sooth have a case of halitosis that could gag a maggot). Several incidents over this three-day period supported, however subtly, my seven-against-one theory. Each of these incidents was apparently isolated. Some of them, I would have been quick to concede, were quite possibly without any nefarious intent or significance. I list them here in sequential order, with subheads to forecast the main players involved in these vignettes. So here we go, beginning with –

Perry

Later on Monday, the day of the weekly meeting, I was passing through the company's reception area. This was a plushly carpeted, softly lighted, and expensively decorated space that served both to impress and intimidate anyone who entered it, particularly first-time visitors such as new-job applicants waiting to be summoned for an interview, business people waiting to be summoned by whomever was their contact within the company, or simply some kid delivering pizzas.

Among the appointments of this area was a grand piano, which no one in the company ever touched . . . except Perry. It was not an unusual sight, especially around lunchtime, to see him either approaching, walking away from, hovering over, or actually playing that piano. Fortunately for all concerned he never played for very long. What he did play was invariable. Perry's repertoire, judging by what I heard, consisted wholly of a series of jazzy-sounding chord changes that he would ham-fistedly pound out, following this racket with a tinkly right-hand flourish on the upper keys.

This activity was but a single element of the jazz-world image of himself that Perry appeared to hold and evidently desired to convey to others, although he did so in a haphazard, or perhaps half-hearted, manner. Overall, Perry was simply not a very jazzy individual. And he was intelligent and self-reflective enough to realize this fact. Nonetheless, from whatever mysterious motives, Perry was willing to settle for a Halloween costume version of Mr Jazz that consisted of a few props, a stereotyped gesture or two, and a plastic mask. Aside from the piano-playing and some talk about the latest CD of jazz music he had purchased, the most conspicuous aspect of Perry's jazzy persona was his eyeglasses, which were the precise type of thick-framed, heavily tinted jobs sported by cool-jazz artists of the 1950s in photographs on the back covers of several prominent record albums of the period. Now, I myself wore eyeglasses (contemporary in design), the lenses of which had a slight amber tint blended into them, although I had opted for this feature on the advice of an optometrist. (I never met an eye doctor or a dentist who wasn't a hustler at heart. Let's not even talk about physicians or – puh! – those bloodletters of the mind with a psychiatric shingle outside their door.) The optometrist suggested that such tinting would better enable my defective sight to tolerate the fluorescent lights of the office as well as the sort of illumination radiated by the screens of televisions and . . . boy, do I hate to even use the word: computers – there, I said it.

As previously mentioned, I was merely passing through the company's reception area. My destination was elsewhere on that floor, where I needed to attend a meeting that concerned some routine function of my job. The piano was so positioned that Perry's jazz-oriented fumblings were being conducted with his back to me as I quietly passed by. So there was no call for me to shout out a hello or disturb the genius jazzer in any way.

But just as I was about to move out of Perry's range, I saw that his head turned to look at me over his shoulder. Of course I couldn't very well have halted in my tracks at that point and acknowledged that I had seen him look at me over his shoulder in what I thought to be a highly devious and menacing way, his eyes fully shaded by the soft lighting of the reception area reflecting off his heavily tinted glasses. At the same moment that he turned his head in my direction, Perry ended his musical performance not with a tinkling flourish on the upper keys of the piano but with a dissonant cluster of notes made by a smash of his left hand on the lowest register of the keyboard. The cacophonous growl of these notes followed me as I made it around a corner and began walking down a long and brilliantly fluorescent hallway on my way to the meeting, which happened to include –

Mary

There she stood some distance down the hallway, only a few feet from the open door of the meeting room, frozen for a second in a pose I had seen her assume before. I thought of it as her 'pre-entry pose', a posture she took on for a fraction of a second during which she seemed to stiffen even more than usual, as if to collect and consolidate herself both mentally and physically before entering a given public forum. Mary was in her fifties and availed herself – from her fluffy-haired head to her pointy high-heels – of all the sartorial and cosmetic armor that was possible for one woman to bear. When viewed in her pre-entry pose, or really at any time when she was not speaking or jotting things in her scheduling book or engaged in some movement or other, she could easily be taken for a mannikin, even at the closest quarters.

Without turning her head toward me – I didn't need that from a mannikin – she entered the meeting room . . . and I followed close behind.

In the course of this meeting, another regular, weekly affair – this one focusing on schedules of production – Mary found the occasion to remark, 'Of course, Frank's department won't be able to meet this deadline,' without qualifying this statement with the reason, which she well knew, for this fact.

'We're still in the process of testing the new software', I explained for the benefit of anyone at the meeting who might not have known why there was a temporary decline in the productivity of my department. The word 'software', as usual, stuck a bit in my throat and came out sounding a bit cracked.

'Of course, we understand,' said Mary while jotting away in her multi-ringed scheduling notebook, not giving the slightest glance my way, as if I had just ineptly attempted to excuse myself and my staff on false grounds.

So the damage, even if it was restricted entirely to atmospherics rather than facts, was done. And well done.

No further encounters took place that day between myself and The Seven – let's just call them that from now on and skip the dwarf part. As far as I'm concerned, fairy tales and legends, mythologies of all times and places, are just festering vestiges of a world that, for better or worse, is dead, dead, dead. Human life is not a *quest* or an *odyssey* or any of that romantic swill which is force-fed to us from our tenderest years to our dying day. All right, then, as Richard, like so many of his intrepid type, would say.

The next run-in I had with one of The Seven didn't occur until the following morning, Tuesday, when I looked up and saw standing at the entrance to my cubicle –

Kerrie

'Do you have any postage stamps you could spare?' she asked. 'I've got to get a credit card payment in the mail pronto.'

I was in the middle of conferring with Lois about the earlier-mentioned software my staff was testing when Kerrie (anorexic and bird-beaked, with a squarish Marine Corps haircut) interrupted us.

'Yeah, I think I've got some,' I said. But what I thought was, 'Why is Kerrie borrowing postage stamps from *me*?' She's the person to whom everyone in the division appeals when they've run out of stamps. The answer, which I heard with one ear as I rummaged through some desk drawers, was rambling out of Kerrie's own mouth.

'Somebody stole all mine. Took a whole roll, not even opened, right out of my desk drawer. I'll have to start hiding the things. Everybody knows where I keep them.'

'Here you go,' I said as I turned in my chair and held out to her a crumpled packet with a few stamps left in it. At the same moment I saw Kerrie pick something up from my cubicle counter.

'Hey, what's this?' she asked, or, more accurately, accused.

What was this indeed, I thought, as I saw Kerrie handling the unopened roll of stamps. Lois, who was seated in a chair between Kerrie and myself, was trying to make herself discreetly invisible by fixing her eyes firmly upon some dimensionless point on the carpet.

'Kerrie,' I said, 'I have no idea where those came from.'

'I just bet you don't, Frank,' said Kerrie before she turned and marched away.

'Lois,' I said, 'did you see those stamps when you came in here?'

Lois materialized from her invisibility and replied, 'No, but I didn't not see them either. I mean, if someone should want to make a big deal about it . . . what could I say?'

'Do you think I might have stolen Kerrie's stamps?'

'Not for a second,' she shot back so fast that her words nearly overlapped my own. 'How could you even ask me that?'

'Sorry,' I said.

'Apology accepted,' said Lois. 'But just because I know you didn't take Kerrie's lousy stamps –'

'Yeah, it looks bad,' I said.

'Yes, it does,' Lois agreed.

That, of course, was exactly why Kerrie made sure that Lois was present as a witness. This enabled Kerrie to say, 'My stamps were missing . . . and I found them on Frank's desk. Go ahead, ask Lois – she was there.' And what could Lois say but, 'Yes, I was there. I saw Kerrie pick up a roll of stamps from Frank's desk.' Of course she could refuse to discuss the subject, but obviously that would only further incriminate me, suggesting not only that Lois witnessed the event but that she also considered it too sordid to speak of. Kerrie had thus crafted a set-up for which I had no possible defense in the Court of Rumor, even if nothing could be positively proved against me.

In contrast to the bold tactics of Kerrie were the effortless subversions of –

Harry

An affable enigma is the only way I can describe him. Always nattily attired, a politely attentive aura hovering somewhere about his person whenever one spoke to him, always willing to 'get right on' things anyone asked him to do, always willing to 'follow through' with things whenever anyone made a request of him ... and never, ever, doing any of these things.

Consequently I was not entirely unnerved when Harry returned none of my phone messages (no one expected to speak to a living Harry when they dialed his extension). It was only when I took Harry's customary black-out on all transmissions coming from me and later added it to Richard's unusual and ominous inattention to my doings throughout the rest of that week, when normally he would have been looking over my shoulder at every opportunity, that I became concerned.

But when it came to matters involving Harry, there was not much of which I could really be sure. What a master in the making he was, even if the truest candidate for better things, faster things, but in no sense cheaper things was –

Barry

He was the most apparent of all the potential heirs to Richard's position when the day came that the one-time star quarterback (or record-breaking baseball pitcher or whatever), for one reason or another, departed from our division, our company, or the world entirely. Seemingly Barry was only passing through on a brief tour of duty as a departmental supervisor in the division. He came to us reputedly as a person who possessed highly evolved organizational skills, which he had demonstrated in a number of other hot-spots throughout the company. When he arrived in our midst he was already widely celebrated – both behind his wide back and to his plump, fast-talking face – for his big brain and his freakish talent for 'sizing things up', for bringing law and order to the company's most unruly frontiers and outposts.

My own sources informed me that the only reason that anyone with whom Barry worked endorsed his gifts so vigorously was to expedite his departure from their precincts, foisting him off on some unsuspecting department that could use some 'revving up' and benefit from the rare potency of his well-endowed frontal lobe. And thus arose the legend of Barry the Brain, Barry the Organizer, and, most unfortunately, Barry the Re-Organizer. Wherever he went in the wildernesses of the company he was given a free hand to revise the charts and maps, the processes and procedures that had always seemed to work so well . . . until he got his meaty hands on them. Because, in fact, as Barry moved with mighty strides from one position to another in the company, he left nothing but chaos, confusion, and conflict in the dust behind him.

In my own observation I could understand how he might be taken for a person of super-developed organizational skills, if only because he showed himself to be cruelly intolerant of the least lack of organization on the part of those around him, using his mile-a-minute mouth, his tireless zest for charts and graphs that no one else could comprehend (due to their over-determined complexity), and his utterly bogus reputation to call into question the qualifications of anyone who questioned his.

Yet there was a time when I actually empathized with this man, who obviously suffered from the same clinical disorder (obsessive-compulsive) with which I myself was plagued, although I struggled to hide my mania, which manifested itself in ways that could not help me in my career, rather than parading it for all to see. But the time for empathy had passed when I arrived at work earlier than usual on Wednesday of that week. I wasn't at all surprised that Barry was in the office at that early hour, although my inner alarm went off when I saw him marauding about the region of my cubicle, moving, as he always did, at a comically brisk pace for a man of his heftiness.

'Barry,' I said by way of greeting.

'Frank,' he returned, his voice dopplering into the distance.

Then, immediately upon entering my cubicle to begin my work that day, I jumped back as if a wild animal had leapt out at me. My own obsessiveness did not involve a fastidious sense of organization, but there was my work-space . . . and it was trim. I didn't think for a moment that the housekeeping staff of the building had gone on a rampage of tidiness where my cubicle was concerned. No others in the area betrayed such treatment, as I noted after a short and secretive investigation.

Okay, so I got the message: 'Barry was here,' it read as if spelled out in pushpins on my bulletin board. What of it? I thought – I had nothing to hide. Then my own variety of obsession took over, and I practically dove for the desk drawer which contained all the electronic and printed documentation of my proposal, my new-product idea, my special plan. I was on my hands and knees staring at the dark metal face of the drawer. I wanted to dust it for fingerprints, use a magnifying glass to examine it for the tiniest signs of forced entry, test with a micrometer if the lock had been tampered with by foreign hands. Of course, none of that would have alleviated my anxiety, and, in time, still on my hands and knees, I finally grasped the handle of the drawer and gave it a heart-stopping pull. It was still locked, for whatever that was worth. And that was worth nothing, because someone could have picked the lock on the drawer, taken its contents, and closed it back up again.

Pulling my wallet from my back pocket and fumbling around for the key, I then opened the drawer. Everything that had been inside before was still inside, yet I nonetheless wanted my print kit, magnifying glass, and micrometer to judge if anything had been disturbed. In addition to the documents locked away in that drawer was a folder of photographs of sites around the city, photographs which I had been taking for years. I had many more such folders at home, full of pictures of alleys and abandoned houses, boarded-up churches, a derelict library (with interior photos of fallen shelves and moldy books strewn across a gritty floor). Most precious to me was a series of photos I took of a place where there stood a crooked street-sign but no longer any street deserving of the name – just some rubble along a path and a few relics of unidentifiable structures on either side of that path.

To the naked eye everything in my desk drawer seemed in order, but it was still possible that Barry had opened the drawer some time before my arrival at work that morning, photocopied the printed version of my document, electronically copied the electronic version of my document, and replaced it with the painstaking precision that only another obsessive could achieve.

'What are you doing down there?' asked the voice of Barry the Detective, Barry the Spy.

I slammed the drawer closed, too afraid to realize that I was giving myself away.

'I was taking something out of my pocket and a quarter popped out. Rolled under my desk.' *Something* out of my pocket? That would not cut it with Barry. It had to be specific. But I did say a *quarter*, not just a coin. 'Did you want something from me?' I asked.

'Yes, I did,' replied Barry in a leisurely manner, uncharacteristically so. He then walked away, also in a leisurely manner.

Barry the Mover, Barry the Shaker.

Barry walked. And talked.

In a *leisurely* manner.

I opened the drawer again and checked its contents, touching the (lousy computer!) disk and rifling through the fiftysome pages of the printed document. Then I locked the drawer. Then I opened the drawer and repeated this ritual as needed throughout the day. I should have taken the goods and gone back home that morning. That would have to wait, though, until the work-day's end. Because, as bad luck would have it, I needed to finish up some small project and pass it on to –

Sherry

I stayed as close to my cubicle as I could during that day. I managed to forego trips to the men's room and went without leaving the building for lunch at the Metro Diner, which was actually a daily pleasure – an escape rather – and not part of any ritualistic behavior. But at some point I needed to pass on this small, this eency-weency project to Sherry. The deadline was two o'clock.

I thought that perhaps I could get Sherry to pick up the work at my cubicle, rather than my having to transport it all the way across the floor to hers. However, she wasn't responding to my phone messages either, nor to the half-hourly messages I sent to her . . . machine.

When the time came to make the delivery I tried to do it as fast as possible, striding at the speed of Barry to Sherry's cubicle, which was near the door leading outside the company's office space and into the hallway, where one could still see the pre-Depression style of the building and enjoy cracked walls and moldings, the dusty globes of dim light that depended from lengthy, tarnished chains running down from the high ceiling, and the creaky railings and banisters that lined the stairwell soaring both upward and downward into the most suggestive shadows I had ever seen.

Arriving at Sherry's cubicle, however, I found that the hand-off was not going to work as smoothly as I hoped.

'Sherry,' I said.

'Could you wait a sec?' she replied, very much preoc-cupied with digging something out of her purse. I realized that it was more than she could handle, taking delivery of this nit-sized project *and* digging something out of her purse. She would have to finish the one before she could turn her mental resources to the other, that's all there was to it.

I declared earlier in this document that, 'with one exception,' there was no cuteness among The Seven. Sherry was the exception, although a serious qualification must be appended to this statement. Physically she was attractive, not to the point of being a harrowing beauty, but enough to put her over the line between women of average or even 'good' looks into the company of those who possessed across-the-room attraction. (If anyone believes that I'm perpetuating some arbitrary or twisted image of the world, that's fine with me – I wish them well in their transactions with social reality.) The qualification to which I made reference above is this: if you happened to cross that room on the other side of which stood Sherry, what you confronted was ... I can't even name it – some kind of *thing* inhabiting the body of an attractive woman, an alien from some diseased planet or a creature of low evolutionary stature that by some curious means had insinuated itself into a human being at some stage in her development, the result being this Sherry-thing.

If she closed her eyes and didn't speak Sherry could indeed pass for an attractive human female. But the moment she spoke or the moment her thing-like eyes came into view, she became a Gorgon (no mythic significance intended or necessary). This duality that Sherry embodied could often be a source of tremendous conflict to those around her, who one moment would experience the tide-pull of her figure and the next moment, when she happened to speak or the image of her eyes loomed up, would be inwardly retching with disgust at the very existence of this Sherry-thing, as well as heaving away inside with self-revulsion for having felt an attraction to this creature. And at the moment I was standing at her desk, Sherry's eyes were turned away from me and I had already forgotten the sound of the few words she had spoken.

So I stood and watched as she dug around for something in her purse, and the deeper she dug the more she shifted about in her chair, causing her already short and close-fitting dress to rise higher and higher toward her buttocks. I was transfixed, turning to stone, until the door leading out into the hallway opened and someone entered the company's office space. This particular someone was Betty, one of the higher vice-presidents in the company. I saw that it was Betty because, having emerged from my fixated staring at Sherry, I now noticed that palmed within her right hand was a small mirror in which she was watching Betty watching me watching her. Sherry then giggled and turned around.

'Hi, Betty,' she said.

'Hello, Sherry,' Betty said.

But Betty had no hellos for Frank after she had seen me looking at Sherry in a way that I never wanted to be seen. Her face merely exhibited a look of disgust (at me!) before she continued on her way.

'Now, what've you got there, Frank?' said Sherry.

Without a word I dropped the folder containing the project on her desk and, for the first time that day, made a visit to the men's room.

5

It was now Friday, and there had been no communication between myself and Richard since Monday. As a formality I decided to check with someone in New Product to confirm whether or not Richard had delivered my truncated version of the two-page proposal that I had shown to The Seven on the first day of that week.

No surprise: New Product had no record of such a proposal with my name attached to it. No surprise: they were no longer even soliciting ideas for New Product and rarely, if ever, did.

No surprise: New Product was as much a mystery to me in its purpose and function as every other division in the company.

Surprise: a 'freeze' had been placed on all activities involving New Product until the upcoming 'restructuring' of the company had been set in motion and the company had 'relocated' its whole operation (more than likely to some nice new high-rise in the suburbs, thereby fleeing the luxuriant rot of the city in which it had resided for over two decades).

While the aforementioned changes within the company were news to me, and big news at that, none of it seemed to have the least force of reality behind it. This was more or less the case with all occasions of 'moment' within that particular working world, and perhaps all others: so often there would be the promise of either some cataclysm or some bright new age on the horizon; but whatever it was, however it might seem to the imagination, it would unfailingly come and go like a thunderstorm through which one had slept, leaving a few puddles and some small tree branches scattered upon the ground as the only evidence that anything at all had happened. Every milestone in the history of the company, even when forecast with heaps of hoopla, was ultimately played out according to some secret timeline of geologic tedium, so that it was drained of all interest and drama well before it took place and afterward went all but unnoticed. And the days rolled by, and one grew older, and none of it seemed to possess the least import or substance. Finally, looking back from the death-bed of your entire life in the working world, you would be left exclaiming, 'What was that all about!' (In this sense the world of the company mirrored the world itself, which sometimes managed to stage a rousing first act, and perhaps even provide a few engaging scenes of a second before devolving into a playwright's nightmare, wherein the actors either butchered their lines or entirely forgot them, scenery collapsed, props misfired, and most of the audience left the theater during intermission.)

Nevertheless, the information that had leaked out to me from New Product served as sufficient excuse to get together over lunch with a friend of mine within the company. (Yes, I did have a friend or two in that place which I have thus far painted so darkly.) I dialed his extension and actually reached a living person on the other end of the line.

'Hey, Frank,' I said. Not only did we share the same given name, but both of us had also labored 'forever,' as one of my staff put it, within our respective departments.

'Yeah, Frank.'

'Got any lunch plans?'

'Do I ever?'

Of course he didn't. Frank kept very much to himself as a rule. Somehow he had managed to remain on an even lower rung of the company ladder than I had over a comparably long ... career, I suppose you would call it. That alone earned him my deep respect. He also knew quite a lot about the company and its personnel that normally would have meant nothing to me.

But that week had been anything but normal, and aside from what I had to tell Frank about the info I acquired from New Product that morning, there was something I wanted to ask him which served as my prime motivation for my requesting a lunchtime audience with my namesake.

I had been waiting outside a few minutes before Frank emerged from the revolving doors of the old building, put on his sunglasses, and lit up a cigarette.

'The usual place?' Frank asked.

'Unless there's somewhere else you'd prefer,' I said.

He just smiled, and we both started walking the mile or so to our destination, weaving through the regular cast of suits and street-people, Frank looking down at the sidewalk as he smoked one cigarette after another while I alternated my gaze between the street level – cheap clothes stores, cheap electronics stores, liquor-lotto-and-checks-cashed-here stores, wig shops, pawn shops, gun shops – and the Beaux-Arts skyline of the ever-receding past.

The Metro Diner was located just beyond the fringes of the central downtown area of the city. When we walked in I looked over toward the counter, behind which stood

Lillian Hayes, the woman who owned and had operated the diner for the past thirty years or so. I caught her eye and smiled, and she gave a little wave my way. Then Frank and I settled into a booth toward the back.

'How's the Sloppy Burger these days?' Frank asked.

'Still sloppy. Still the best.'

'That's for me, then,' he announced as he stubbed out his cigarette in a crusted ashtray that had a little metal band arching over it with grooves in which lighted cigarettes could be secured. 'You don't see these things much any more,' Frank observed, examining the ashtray with the eye of the most sensitive lover of downtrodden artifacts. 'There's something about it, you know?'

'I know,' I said. 'There's a Japanese word for it – *wabi*.'

'Wa-BEE,' repeated Frank, who didn't require a verbal definition of the word to understand its meaning.

There was a lot about the Metro Diner that shared this same quality, which was the primary reason I had been an habitué of the place for many years. I also lived in the backstairs apartment above the diner, for which Lillian charged me a modest monthly rent.

Over our Sloppy Burgers I told Frank about the restructuring of the company I had heard about, which elicited from him only a shrug of profound uninterest. Then I told him about the relocation, which interested him only from the practical standpoint of travel-time to and from work.

'Is that it?' Frank asked.

'Not quite,' I said.

'What? Somebody die?'

'No,' I said.

'You're leaving the company. Great.'

'No, I'm not leaving the company, Frank.'

'Then what?' he asked.

'A question,' I said with a deliberate gravity that Frank just as deliberately ignored.

'Okay, shoot.'

'Frank, why is Richard called The Doctor?'

Frank smiled and pushed aside the plate on which only a few ketchup-soaked fries remained. Then he slowly, almost ritualistically lit up a cigarette.

'This is going to cost you lunch, you know that, don't you?'

'Done,' I agreed.

'You really don't know about this? I mean, if you know that Richard's called The Doctor in the first place, you should know the reason why.'

'Well, I don't. I'm not even sure how I know what I know. I think I overheard it somewhere. Maybe it's a false memory, I don't know. But my feeling is that this is not something I should be asking just anybody at the company.'

'You're right about that,' Frank said. 'You ask the wrong person what you just asked me and you might end up on your way out.'

'Yeah, I understand that there've been people who were fired for one reason or another because of Richard. So he's a PhD in office politics – that much I know.'

'Wrong. The title of "doctor" is ironic,' Frank explained. 'Here's the reason. Richard has no fewer than three suicides to his credit – two women, one guy. I can't believe you don't know this.'

'You know me, Frank. I keep my head in the sand. It feels good down there.'

'I know, "Stay stupid, stay alive",' Frank said. 'But that motto doesn't apply when it comes to Richard. I knew the family of the guy who *did* himself. He actually named Richard in his suicide note, but there was nothing that the family could do – legally, I mean. He was a head case to begin with anyway. One of the women who killed herself didn't leave a note, but it wasn't hard to put cause and effect together. Rumor was she had had an affair with Richard. This was back when he was in ... whatever division he was in before he came to live with us.'

'And the other woman?' I asked.

Frank paused to light another cigarette. 'This is the best one. It happened a couple months before you started at the company. This chick slit her wrists right in Richard's office. Died spread out over his desk, blood running everywhere.'

'Like a dead patient on an operating table.'

'Right. It was that one that got him the name The Doctor. Before that little incident the guy was in line to become CEO. He should have been running the company a long time ago. Who knows where he'd be now? Definitely not the manager of our hole-in-the-wall division. Even the other suicides wouldn't have made any difference. If anything they only enhanced his résumé as a real powerhouse exec. But the dead girl in the office – that didn't look too good.'

'I think we'd better head back,' I said, looking at my watch.

On the way out I waved goodbye to Lillian, and she waved back to me.

'Frank, I hope you didn't ask me about Richard because you're having some problem with him,' said Frank as we retraced our route back to the building.

At the time I could neither confirm nor deny that this was the case.

6

There are some people who attest that they do not remember their dreams, who have never known what it's like to awake screaming or half-insane or merely trembling from the aftershock of a nightmare. These are not necessarily simple-minded persons or happy persons or persons of stunted imaginations. But somehow they have retained a lifelong innocence, never knowing the dread some feel upon approaching the bedroom and facing that descent into the darkness of unknown worlds that may range from cartoonish absurdity to quaking horror. They are very lucky people. I wish I were one of them.

Over the weekend I tried to put the office out of my mind like a

Bad Dream

This task was made considerably more difficult by the new nightmares that began visiting me, ones in which a sleep-world version of Richard took center stage. In these dreams I found myself back at the company, a place that resembled the dimestore I used to visit when I was a kid.

In the real dimestore there was a corner that served as a miniature pet shop where living merchandise was on display. Several aquariums held a variety of small fish, and terrariums featured chameleons or tar-colored reptiles of some type that lay motionless against the glass. Parakeets twittered in bell-shaped cages, while guinea pigs and gerbils scampered about in square, smelly cages. I was walking slowly up and down the aisles, in my dimestore nightmares, fearful of drawing attention to myself. The reason I walked so slowly was that the floors were made of soft slats of wood which creaked with every step I took, and I didn't want to be seen by Richard, who was over in the corner with the caged animals.

He was doing something terrible to them, although I couldn't specify what it was.

But his fingers were able to reach between the closely spaced bars of the cages and could penetrate the glass of the fish tanks and the terrariums. I wanted to know what he was doing to these animals, but I was too afraid to look. And there were voices whispering to me about Richard. 'He's fixing them,' the voices said, answering the unspoken question in my fearful mind. 'Why is he called The Doctor?' I asked aloud, addressing no one. 'He's here to fix them,' the voices reiterated, as if somehow meaning both to reassure and to frighten me at the same time.

I wanted to run out of the store, but the front entrance through which I had entered was now only a blank wall.

The only way out was through the back door in the corner where Richard was occupied with the animals. He seemed fairly engrossed in whatever horrible things he was doing, and I thought that if I could run fast enough I could make it past him and escape through the back. When I finally reached my destination, fighting my way through the resistant atmosphere of the dream dimestore, I found that the doors were locked. I tried to kick the doors open, but then I saw that their glass was reinforced by criss-crossing veins of metal wire. Before I woke up screaming, Richard turned his head to look my way and then reached out to grab me. But his hands weren't hands. They were

Great White Gloves

But these gloves didn't have the requisite number of fingers on them. I had seen them before . . . and not just in dreams. Because nothing in dreams is original; it's all plagiarized from waking life. And the gloves in the dream were merely a frightening reflection of something I had come upon earlier that Saturday afternoon.

There was a derelict warehouse that was located just outside the downtown area. For some time I had intended to make an excursion there in order to look around inside and take some photographs before the city had the place sealed up. I was not in any sense an expert photographer, and my equipment was not in the least sophisticated or expensive. I took my pictures in color – not the black-and-white of a serious photographic artist – and brought my film to a local drugstore for processing.

While I certainly desired to retain a record of the sites I had visited around the city over the years, my picture-taking was something of an excuse to justify and explain (both to myself and to anyone else who might wonder) my presence in the city's many regions that had passed from squalor to abandonment, from abandonment to decay, and from decay into the ultimate stages of degeneration that bordered upon complete disappearance from this world. It was not the *wabi* of battered but still useful objects that I was seeking; it was the *sabi* of things utterly dejected and destitute, alone and forgotten – whatever was submitting to its essential impermanence, its transitory nature, whatever was teetering on the brink of non-existence that was the fate of everything that had ever been and awaited everything that would ever be . . . every person, every place, every purpose, and every plan that could possibly be conceived. This, in a nutshell, was what brought me to explore, and to photographically document, the exterior shell and the interior spaces of a derelict warehouse that Saturday afternoon.

This place was not unlike many others to which I had made similar excursions. From outside one couldn't say for sure what purpose the structure, which occupied almost half a city block (not including the field of weeds and broken concrete adjacent to the building), had once served. The words painted across its side had been reduced by time and the elements to a few fragmented letters which themselves had all but found their way to the other side of invisibility. But I had already gained enough experience in these matters to be able to distinguish a derelict *factory* from a derelict *warehouse*. And once inside, entering through a doorway without a door, I found that I was correct in my judgment.

I should say that it was not my customary practice as an aficionado of modern ruins to invade their interiors. There were several good reasons for this.

One: there were physical risks when one disturbed the sensitive spaces of deteriorating structures – every footstep had the potential of setting off a chain reaction of collapsing walls, stairways, overhead fixtures, and the like.

Two: these places frequently served as home-ground for various persons who had nowhere else to call home, the cast-offs and losers of a world that had no use for them and did everything it could to push them further and further into exile, because the presence of these living ghosts, these ambulatory spirits, was simply too haunting to be tolerated, provoking a dismal reminder of something that must be ignored at all costs ... for these specters were not merely human detritus that the rest of us had left behind, but also citizens of a future that awaits all the empires infesting this earth, not to mention the imminent fall of those fragile homelands of flesh which we each inhabit. And even though I already had taken several psychological steps into their desperate world, I felt too much fear of these precocious residents of oblivion to advance any further.

Three: the sad and tranquil pleasures of *sabi* that lured me to these old piles were best enjoyed at a distance, in suggestive long-shot views of desolate scenes rather than too-clear close-ups of some hopeless drunk or drug addict urinating against a wall.

Yet there are some structures that draw you into them, inviting you inside to wallow in their degraded wonders. From the first time I visited the site of this derelict warehouse, which I had already photographed from the outside, I knew that this was one of those places, if only because its exterior offered so little in the way of outward suggestiveness – a nameless shell whose history and hopes were held back from the outside observer. It all seemed so enticing, but like every other attraction along the world's midway the greatest part of its appeal lay in those moments of anticipation. And after it was all over, the particular attraction which had once promised so much would send you on your way unrewarded, purged of your curiosity and the poorer for being so. This derelict warehouse was, of course, no different.

At least there were no squatters inside that I was called upon to deal with, or none that I saw. And the structure was still fairly safe and solid, with steel stairways that hadn't come loose from their walls, allowing me to make a quick reconnaissance of the place from bottom to top. Aside from the usual array of refuse and junkyard leavings – liquor bottles, worn-out tires, parts of machines, parts of appliances, parts of parts – I did find a filing cabinet in a room on the uppermost floor of the warehouse. Within that cabinet's drawers there were a few pages from a receipt pad that bore the ink-stamped imprint of Murphy's Costumes and Theatrical Supplies, a business that evidently stored some of its eponymous inventory in the warehouse. After further investigation I found some items lying in the dirt and darkness of a shattered wall. These were: (1) a couple of mannikin hands, both lefties, and (2) a very dirty pair of oversized gloves, each with a set of *four* sausage-shaped fingers – the accurate but strangely impractical accoutrements for the outfitting of both amateurs and professionals called upon to impersonate a beloved and begloved cartoon star. How mysterious, how ridiculous, that my dreaming brain would discard the dismembered mannikin hands, which I found intriguing enough to take back home with me, and decide to feature in my nightmare about Richard those unnaturally large gloves, which I left behind as lesser mementos of that disappointing warehouse excursion.

Walking back to my apartment, I passed through the many shadows cast by great hotels, movie theaters, department stores, and office towers, each of them once filled to capacity with dreams of a future that abandoned them all with an unforeseen haste, leaving behind only untended monuments in a cemetery that no one bothered to visit any more – with the exception of the odd photographer of ruins. Twilight shone through the spaces between these structures and illuminated their soaring peaks with an amber light, the hue of setting suns and fading worlds.

The particular night that followed would have one hour removed from it, as the time zone in which I lived had 'daylight savings' forced upon it, which for me only meant that I would spend the rest of that spring, all of summer, and five weeks of fall trying to recover a lost hour of sleep. This scheme for *saving daylight* – for creating the illusion that we could manipulate the clockwork movements of our solar system – was once justified to me as being 'good for business'. Before returning to my apartment, I stopped by the Metro Diner to put this matter before –

Lillian

'Good for *business*?' she repeated with the emphasis of a skeptic. 'That's news to this old gal. You see anyone else besides you sitting at my counter?' (Lillian commonly referred to the diner as a whole with the synecdoche of 'her counter'.) 'You think another hour of sunshine is going to make any difference to me? Maybe it does to other folks, I don't know.'

As Lillian was talking to me she was staring at the two mannikin hands that I had set down on the stool next to me. She reached under the counter and produced one of the brown bags that the diner used to package carry-out orders. 'Would you do me the favor of putting those nasty things where I can't see them,' she said, handing me the bag.

'Sorry, Lil,' I said as I stuffed the plaster hands inside the bag and crumpled it closed. But I wasn't sure if my apology was for thoughtlessly bringing these unclean objects into Lillian's otherwise well-scrubbed place of business or if the sight of these replicant parts of the human body somehow unsettled her. I suspected it was the latter, but I didn't pursue the issue.

'You still taking pictures of those old buildings and junk for your book?' Lillian asked.

'Mm-hm,' I wordlessly replied, turning away to look out the front window of the diner. I found it difficult, almost painful, to perpetuate the lie of 'my book' to Lillian. But what could I say to her? That I'm drawn to those old buildings and junk because (voice beginning to seethe) . . . because they take me into a world (the seething builds) . . . a world that is the exact opposite of the one (voice seething to a pitch) . . . the one I'm doomed by my own weakness and fear to live in (uncontrollable, meta-maniacal seething)

... to live in during my weeks, my months, my years and years of work ... work ... work?

'I don't understand it,' she said. 'There's so many pretty things you could be taking pictures of. Far as that goes, I still don't know why you live upstairs – not saying I ain't glad to have a regular-paying tenant. But even I live in a better neighborhood. And *you* could live anywhere you want.'

'What can I say, Lil? I am addicted to your cooking. Speaking of which, could I get the meatloaf special before you close for the day?'

'Sure can,' Lillian replied as she lit up a cigarette. 'You hear that, Rudy?'

'Yeah, I heard,' the voice of Rudy called out.

As she poured out two cups of coffee (decaf for me, as she already knew), I wondered if Lillian's employees feared her in the way that I feared Richard. After all, one business is essentially the same as another, and she was the owner, CEO, and sole stockholder of that longstanding enterprise called the Metro Diner. I judged her to be easily as tough as Richard, and, in her own world, just as savvy. Was I now trading pleasantries with an elderly black woman who beneath the surface was no different from Richard the Bastard, Richard the Evil One? I liked Lillian, but I knew her only from the perspective of the customer, which made me just a little current in that river of cash that she needed to keep flowing into her accounts.

'You going to just stare at that coffee?' Lillian asked.

I smiled at being caught in an unguarded state of preoccupation with my dark thoughts. Then I took a sip of the decaf.

'It's good. Tastes like the real thing,' I said, and this time I was telling the truth.

'Nothing hard about making a good cup of coffee,' Lillian said to this customer as she lit up another cigarette.

And that statement provided something of an answer to my questions about Lillian and her business. Because the coffee at the Metro Diner didn't have to be as good as it was, nor did the excellent food served there have to be so carefully prepared or so reasonably priced. That was not how we did things where I happened to work. The company that employed me strived only to serve up the cheapest fare that its customers would tolerate, churn it out as fast as possible, and charge as much as they could get away with. If it were possible to do so, the company would sell what all businesses of its kind dream about selling, creating that which all our efforts were tacitly supposed to achieve: the ultimate product – Nothing. And for this product they would command the ultimate price – Everything.

This *market strategy* would then go on until one day, among the world-wide ruins of derelict factories and warehouses and office buildings, there stood only a single, shining, windowless structure with no entrance and no exit. Inside would be – will be – only a dense network of computers calculating profits. Outside will be tribes of savage vagrants with no comprehension of the nature or purpose of the shining, windowless structure. Perhaps they will worship it as a god. Perhaps they will try to destroy it, their primitive armory proving wholly ineffectual against the smooth and impervious walls of the structure, upon which not even a scratch can be inflicted.

I spent most of my days in a world devoted to turning this fable into a reality, I knew that. I also knew that the Metro Diner did *not* exist in that world, that somehow it was located in another place altogether, a zone where the daylight really had been saved, even if it was fast running out. That was why I liked Lillian; that was why I lived in the apartment above her diner. And that, alas, was why I began dreaming about The Doctor who reached with his puffy, four-fingered gloves into the cages and tanks of animals, of living merchandise, in a dimestore pet shop.

Monday morning I awoke before dawn, shaking from the effects of another of these dreams.

'He has special gloves for fixing them,' I mumbled with dream-horror. 'He can go inside with his gloves.'

Even then he was already inside me, just as he had been inside so many others before ... fixing them, fixing and fixing, fixing until – in one way or another – they broke.

7

All right, then!

But I didn't have the opportunity to hear Richard speak these words that Monday. When I entered the room where I and The Seven gathered according to a weekly schedule, where we sat in the dried-up leather of enormous chairs at a scarred-up banquet table, our little voices droning amid great dim spaces decorated in a Victorian Gothic style, I saw that the meeting was already in progress.

'Look who decided to join us,' Richard bellowed as I closed the heavy and intricately carved door of the room behind me. 'Glad you could make it, Mr Domino.'

I glanced at my watch, which I had had the habit of obsessively monitoring for as long as I could remember. I had not arrived late to the meeting. 'I didn't know the time of the meeting had been pushed back,' I said as I took my seat, everyone else staring at me in silence.

'Is it "pushed back" or "moved forward"?' Richard asked rhetorically ... and disingenuously. 'I can never keep those straight.'

'It's pushed back, I'm pretty sure,' said Sherry, giving the answer to a question that she didn't realize needed none.

'Well, in plain English, the time of the meeting was changed,' said Richard, shifting back to his usual voice of bland authority. 'You should read your messages, Domino.'

'I did. There was no message about –'

'Actually, Richard,' interrupted Kerrie, 'I didn't want to risk someone not showing up on time because they didn't read their messages promptly, so I went around and personally told everyone ... including Frank.'

It made sense that Kerrie the Framer of Innocent Persons for Stealing Her Lousy Stamps would have the job of insuring that I arrived late to the meeting. There was no point in contradicting her. She could lie far better than I could tell the truth. But that wasn't what worried me at the moment. The greater issue was that The Seven had held a secret meeting before the real meeting. And I would never know what was on that other meeting's agenda.

'Well, never mind that now,' said Richard as though he were giving me a reprieve. 'We've wasted enough time on this already. Let's just move on to the usual reports and rigmarole. I'll bring Frank up to speed on the rest of it later.'

It was another full hour before the meeting ended. By that time everyone had drained to the dregs their two-liter-sized bottles of water, their waxy containers of fruit juice, and their volcano-shaped cups of coffee, tea, or who knows what. (I could still feel the single cup of decaf I'd consumed with breakfast at the Metro Diner sloshing around inside me.) Even Richard had upended his tall thermos of coffee, shaking it over his mug to get at those refractory few drops at the bottom. That was something I had never seen before, which led me to wonder how long the rest of them had been in conference before I arrived. Of course no mention was made of my new product idea, my special plan. That whole matter had entered a realm of gamesmanship that now concerned only Richard and me, and had nothing at all to do with the company . . . or with my original intentions to reaffirm my unity with The Seven Swine.

After the meeting concluded, the other six supervisors gathered up their ringed scheduling books along with their cups, bottles, and waxy boxes, and filed out of the room in total silence, leaving me and Richard sitting some distance away from each other at that long banquet table. Richard was still shuffling some papers around and scribbling in his own scheduling book, or rather *books*, plural, while I waited anxiously for him to 'bring me up to speed'. He reigned supreme when it came to the art of the torturous stall, creating the sense of a waiting period that might just trail off into eternity. Then, suddenly, he arranged his papers in a neat stack, slammed both of his notebooks closed, and looked down the table at Domino, who was rolling his pencil back and forth in an attempt to appear calm and casual, even bored. But I botched it, because as soon as Richard was ready to talk I brought that pencil-rolling to an instant halt and jerked my neck around to face the man at the head of the table.

'This is how it is, Frank,' he began. 'There's going to be a few changes, sort of a shifting around. Barry's going to be leaving our little group in order to head up a committee to come up with a proposal for the new restructuring of the company, which we all knew was coming. It's Barry's wish that you also serve on this committee – quite a compliment, I would say, considering the source. Now this is only a temporary arrangement, but it's going to be a full-time job. You, Barry, and several others to be named later will need to fully draft your proposal by midsummer. This timetable comes straight from the crowd upstairs. They want to see the new restructuring in place by year's end.'

'Can I ask the purpose of the new restructuring?'

'You know. It's the same theme as the last restructuring. I mean, sweet Jesus, how many variations can there be on cheaper, faster, and . . . that other thing?' Richard was as skilled as ever in privately sharing his very genuine cynicism in order to create the false sense that he was really on your side. 'But if I were you, I wouldn't bring up questions like that in front of the others on the committee. Just follow Barry's lead. He knows what's what with these things.'

'And what happens in the meantime, while Barry and I are serving full-time on this committee?'

'Mary's going to take over the day-to-day supervision of Barry's department, in addition to her own. And Kerrie will do the same thing with respect to your people. She knows quite a bit about that new software being tested in your department. It's only a temporary arrangement. I don't foresee any bumps along the way. Do you?'

'None at all,' I agreed, not bothering to bring up Kerrie's militaristic style of management, her burgeoning psychosis, and her all-round demonic nature.

For the next few months I served – under Barry – on the restructuring committee, trying to make sense of his concepts for a company-wide reorganization and wearily accepting the successive editions of what he called The Master Chart, which even in its earliest stages resembled a more densely wrought and diabolical version of Dante's map of Hell. Barry handed out these revised charts to the rest of us almost on a daily basis. Each one contained some infinitesimal modification or addition to the one before it, until the pages outlining his brainchild of restructuralization were almost black with boxes filled with tiny letters that had arrows pointing upward, downward, and sideways to other boxes filled with tiny letters. I never read any of the words – at least I assumed they were words – formed by those tiny letters, which grew tinier and tinier as the boxes became increasingly more numerous and the arrows (the arrows!) ultimately pointed in every direction. Finally the deadline arrived for the committee to turn over its proposal to the greater powers whose offices occupied the twentieth (twenty-first?) floor of the pre-Depression-era building in which the company was located ... until the time would come for it to relocate to a suburban locale far from the taxes of the city's downtown area. Now I could return to my old job as a department supervisor – right?

Wrong: Because under Kerrie's management two of my old staff had transferred to another division, two had left the company, and two had been fired.

Wrong: Because Kerrie had her staff, 'Kerrie's Special Forces' she called them, doing all the work once done by both my staff and hers.

(Barry didn't return as the supervisor of his old department either, but that was the way things were supposed to work out. He would start working on Phase Two of the company-wide restructuring, while his staff was integrated with Kerrie's Special Forces. Two understaffed departments were now doing the work of three that had been fully staffed. If I had only paid closer attention to Barry's charts I might have noticed that this merging of 'work cells' was part of the company's restructuring.)

And wrong again: Because I had been given a new role in the company's puppet show, and Richard was pulling the strings with the four, surgically dexterous, fingers of his great gloved hands.

8

By the end of the summer I was sitting in one of Barry's tiny square boxes in a corner of the company far removed from where I had been just a few months before. My coworkers were now temporary help, college co-ops, and persons who possessed the ability to spend every workday with their eyes positioned eighteen inches from a glaring _____ screen, their fingertips in constant motion across their keyboards, a never-diminishing pile of pages stacked on the desk counter beside them.

On the rare occasions that I ran into one of The Seven – perhaps in a lavatory, perhaps in a hallway – they never failed to greet me with the sweetest smiles and concerned inquiries into 'how I was doing'.

'Just fine,' I replied, although my unsmiling face and dead voice gave me away to The Victorious Seven, who were on the side of righteousness, the rule of corporate law, and Richard. Speaking of whom, I should record the fact that every so often I still received messages from him asking about my new-product idea and suggesting that perhaps the time was nigh for the company to make some riskier moves.

Was he serious? I didn't know. Did he want to use the complete documentation of my idea, my special plan, to undermine my status in the company even further than he already had? Or was there some other reason altogether that he kept up communications with me on this subject? I didn't know, I didn't know. But I did know one thing: no good could come of giving Richard what he wanted from me. He would never, ever see the full documentation of my idea, because it was now in a very safe place. And withholding what Richard wanted did give me some minuscule satisfaction that mitigated, however slightly, what I had endured at the hands of The Seven.

So why did I stand for such treatment? Why didn't I leave the company? Why didn't I do any of a dozen things that I had contemplated doing for many years?

At the time there was only one answer to these questions. The Doctor had gone inside me, and with his gloved hands he had fixed me and fixed me good. Did I mention that I suffered from Obsessive-Compulsive Disorder?

Even for a person of average emotional stability the lust for revenge can be quite a time-consuming affair. For me it was all-consuming. It shoved aside every other thought that got in its way, every fantasy and feeling that might have led me back to my former self, every memory of who or what I had ever been. My nights and weekends were now taken over by a set of constantly recycled scenarios in which Domino had his day. And that day was soaked in bathtubs of blood, a day of judgment overseen by a never-setting sun that burned madly red against a black sky.

But I had always been weak, and, as I think I might also have mentioned, I had always been afraid. So Domino would tough it out, Domino would hang in there, Domino would lay low until . . . until . . . until *what* I had no idea. Until . . .

One night I was preparing to leave work, putting away my ID badge, shutting down that staring square of the _____, etc. And, obsessive-compulsive that I am, I had gotten into the habit of placing a page from a legal pad on top of my pile of unentered data, a page on which I had written 'WORK NOT DONE', just in the unlikely event, just on the remotest chance, that someone from the cleaning staff, or who-knows-who, might see this pile of data as the wastepaper which, in fact, it could justly be mistaken for. No one else among my coworkers, it goes without saying, ever took such precautions. I, on the other hand, could not maintain that puny part of serenity that I still enjoyed without doing so.

But when I arrived at my desk the next morning, my WORK NOT DONE note, along with the whole pile of unentered data it covered, was gone, nowhere to be found, disappeared. I reported the missing materials to my supervisor, who, strangely enough, did not seem in the least concerned with its whereabouts.

'What really concerns me, Frank,' said this boy who a year before had not even heard of the company in which he now held the post of supervisor, 'that is, my primary concern, is your overall performance, both in this department and in the company as a whole. You're the least productive employee in the department, for one thing. And I've been looking at your file from Human Resources. It's kind of ugly, if you want to know the truth. Forget that you've never really been a team player, at least according to the evaluations you've gotten from your former manager. There's also stuff here about theft from other employees, mismanaging your department when you were a supervisor, not carrying your weight when you served on the restructuring committee, sexual harassment, an overall lacksa–lackadais– a bad attitude. It's your whole profile that's the problem. I've tried to cut you some slack around here because I know you've been with the company for a long time. But you're just dead weight these days. This so-called disappearance of your work – I don't know what to make of *that*. Someone's going to have to go to a lot of trouble to regenerate that data. I'm thinking that maybe that's what you wanted.'

After continuing in this vein for a while longer, my punk of a supervisor gave me the option of resigning from the company, which I did immediately. I didn't want to, I really didn't. But there was no other choice. I knew who was behind this business, and I didn't stand a chance against him.

Before I cleaned out my desk – which was not a big deal since the only personal possessions I now kept at work were some packages of cookies – and before I turned in my letter of resignation (Why letter? Why not statement . . . or declaration?), I stopped by the men's room and simply stood before the large mirror, staring at the image of someone who was staring back at me.

He was of average height and build, average weight, average age, with hair neither long nor short. He was clean-shaven. He wore corrective lenses with a slight amber tint. His eyes were brown.

'All right, then,' he said to the image in the mirror. Then he turned and walked out of the room.

9

Cheap clothes stores, cheap electronics stores, liquor-lotto-and-checks-cashed-here stores, wig shops, pawn shops, gun shops . . . gun shops . . . gun shops.

There was a particular gun shop that I walked by every day on my route to and from my job. It was a small building and never appeared to be open for business. I had never been in a gun shop before, but I walked into this one as if I were a regular customer. Looking around I felt the same excitement I'd known as a kid when I visited the local dimestore to run my eyes over the colorful boxes of model cars, the battery-operated robots, the squirt guns, the cap guns, the cowboy guns, the tommy guns.

'What can I do for you?' asked the bearded little man, almost a dwarf, who emerged from a back room. I must not have answered him, because he repeated his question. Then he said, 'Are you looking to buy a firearm?'

'Yes, sir,' I said emphatically. 'Indeed I am.'

'Something for personal protection?' asked the bearded little man.

'Actually,' I said, 'I'm here for a dual purpose. *Personal* protection is in fact an issue. You see, the neighborhood where I live isn't as safe as it might be.'

'I hear you,' interjected the bearded man who seemed to have lost about an inch in height since he first appeared.

'Yes, well, that's the first part of my mission. The second is that I'm here to do some early Christmas shopping. I have some friends, seven of them to be exact. And this year I'd like to present them with the gift, as you say, of personal protection.'

'I've done the same myself.'

'Really,' I said, noticing that the gun-shop dwarf had definitely shrunk another half inch or so. 'Now I have to admit that I'm not very familiar with all the varieties of handguns – you have quite a lot of them here.'

'Best selection in the downtown area.'

'That's terrific. Then show me what you've got. I'm very much open to suggestions.'

But the dwarf had disappeared entirely from sight. Then I saw that he had only been squatting down with his head inside the glass counter that stood between us. When he stood up – no bigger than before and perhaps even a bit more shrunken – he held out a handgun that looked absolutely gargantuan in his puny palm.

'Go ahead – hold it.'

I did.

'It's a Glock,' he said.

'I've heard of these from television shows,' I said, amazed at how wonderful it felt in my hand. I pointed it toward the wall and looked down the barrel. Tears almost came to my eyes. In the background of my elation the dwarf spoke of the weapon's reliability ... its accuracy ... its magazine capacity!

'I'm sold. I'll take two of these – one for myself and one for my friend Barry. What else have you got?'

The dwarf began rushing around. He was now so close to the floor that I had to look over the counter to see him. He showed me Rugers, he showed me Mausers, he showed me Smiths, Brownings, and Berettas. And then he showed me a Firestar.

'Compact, nice weight. You could carry it around in your jacket and not even know it was there. Has a seven-round capacity.'

'Seven,' I repeated. And in the next breath put it on my shopping list for Sherry. 'It should fit perfectly into a woman's purse, wouldn't you say?'

'I suppose. If the purse wasn't one of those tiny things.'

After seeing a few more makes and models of handguns on which I had to pass, feeling myself an expert at this stage, the dwarf brought forth a USP Tactical.

'Forty-five automatic. Five-inch barrel for superior accuracy. A real special forces weapon.'

'Did you say "special forces"?' I said.

He did.

'Do you have a couple of them in stock?'

He did, a blessing on his dwarfish head.

That left two more to complete my arsenal. And I knew just what I wanted. Their barrel lengths, it turned out, were only one inch and seven-eighths.

'Uncle Mike's Boot, they're called,' said the dwarf. 'Fits right into an ankle holster, just like you said you wanted.'

'And do you have such holsters readily available?' I asked.

'I can get them by the time the legal paperwork goes through on this merchandise.'

'Do the holsters come in black?' I asked.

'I can check. Do you want holsters for the rest?'

'Yes, I do. And make sure there's one left-side holster for my lefty friend Perry.'

The truth was that, among my other unusual traits, I was ambidexterous. And the cinematic image of a vengeful figure pulling out pistols with both hands at once suddenly flickered brightly in my brain.

'Holsters are important for safety reasons,' squeaked a voice from the shadows of the floor. 'I've also got the kind that clip onto your belt.'

'That's exactly what I was thinking,' I said as I laid my credit card down on the counter and began filling out the registration forms. 'By the way, is there possibly a place in the nearby area where I could get some instruction in the proper use of firearms?'

It so happened there was. So my schedule was set. I could pick the guns up on Friday and then spend some time working on my weapons technique. By Monday morning I would be ready.

As I was filling out the last of the registration forms I happened to glance at another section of the counter where a shining array of outdoor knives was laid out. One in particular caught my eye.

'Thirteen-inch Buck Skinner Hunting Knife,' the dwarf informed me.

'That is excellent,' I gasped, trying my hardest not to weep with gratitude at the magnificence of this implement.

Farewell to the humble charms of *wabi*, the morose pleasures of *sabi*. Greetings to the potent joy of cold-forged steel . . . to the harsh intoxications of temperature-resistant polymer components . . . and a special hello to pure ballistic stopping power.

'Your credit card is really taking a pounding today,' said the bearded little man, who had returned to his previous height.

'Oh, that's all right,' I said, picking up my bag containing my leather-sheathed Buck Skinner Hunting Knife. I had already made my last payment to those bloodsuckers who had issued me that particular piece of plastic, I thought as I stepped out of the gun shop and into the sunshine of a brilliant October afternoon. But I had a busy day ahead, and no time to waste.

10

I skipped lunch and went directly to the only halfway decent men's clothiers with a franchise still located downtown. There was a metal plaque flanking the entrance to the store which told me that the clothes company had been founded the same year that young Mary Shelley published the first edition of her novel *Frankenstein* (1818). What a glad coincidence that I happened to be looking for an outfit in the gothic style.

I purchased one light and loose-fitting raincoat (color: black), one mock turtleneck that was made mostly of Italian Merino wool (color: black), one pair of black denim pants that fit nicely over a pair of black leather boots and provided plenty of room to secrete those boot guns named for good old Uncle Mike. (And those holsters better be black, I thought.) I was wearing my new clothes when I walked out of the store, having abandoned my old ones in the dressing room. I asked to keep the box for the boots, since I would need it when I proceeded directly to my bank in order to empty my savings account.

'May I ask why you've decided to close your account with us?' asked the gray-suited man to whom the teller had sent me. He was sitting behind a desk in a corner of the great vaulted lobby of the bank.

'Because I despise you,' I replied, looking at him straight in the eye from behind amber-tinted eyeglasses.

'I beg your pardon?'

'I think you heard me. This is a bank. I'd rather carry my money around in my crotch than have it serve the purposes of this institution for another minute.'

The banker, somewhat petulantly, retrieved three forms from the top drawer of his desk and asked me to fill them out. Two of the forms he kept. The third he told me to take to the teller who had sent me to him. 'This is a waiver. You understand that the bank can't be held responsible for cash withdrawals once you've taken possession of your funds. Even while you're still on the bank's premises, our security guards will not be available for your protection.' As I rose to go back to the teller's window and have all my money loaded into the shoe box I had brought with me, the gray-suited man added, 'We *sincerely* have enjoyed serving you and hope to do so again in the future.' It occurred to me that all civilization was structured so that such people could make snide remarks like that and get away with it. They had been getting away with it for thousands of years and would continue to get away with it until the end of time.

After cashing out at the bank, I took the shoe box back to my apartment and wrapped it securely with packing tape. Then with a felt-tip pen I wrote across the top: 'For Lillian Hayes. Thank you.' I signed my name underneath these words, along with the day's date. Then I placed the box on my desk between my computing machine and printer.

Yes: I did own such a machine, despite the maledictions I routinely heaped upon them. (I told Richard I had worked on my new-product idea at home, and that was the truth. I only lied about having any part of it in hand-written form.)

No: I wasn't going to take an ax or a baseball bat to it.

Yes: I did plan to take an ax or a baseball bat to it when the time came.

But until then I still had use for it. Before I did what I was going to do, I needed to make a statement, because I had no intention of being around for questioning when the smoke cleared. And there were definite issues that needed to be addressed.

First: *The question of insanity*. This would certainly be a discourse that would eat up quite a few pages. However ludicrous it now sounds to me, at the time I was quite concerned that in the aftermath of things I would not be dismissed as just another kook. A loner who took pictures of ruined places in his spare time. A burned-out weirdo. A guy who couldn't take the pressure and who finally 'snapped' like so many others before him. Even worse – to be perceived as a psychological casualty of *the times*, as if there were something special about any period, any place in which a particular body chanced to find itself in motion. I must have been crazy to have thought I could talk my way out of that one!

Second: *The issue of evil*. For many years, as I ran my mind's eye over the tiny print of the innumerable pages of history ... or contemplated some great (or not so great) atrocity reported by the nightly news, I always said to myself: 'Better to be the one who is executed than the one who performs the execution.' I knew that I would have to come up with some fancy reasoning to maneuver myself from that position of armchair rectitude to a pile of bullet-shredded bodies, even if the last one on the heap was my own. Many, many words would have to be processed and many pages printed out to explicate such a dramatic moral turnaround. Or so it seemed to me as I walked the floor of my apartment, tapping out a rhythm on my black-denim-clad leg with the blade of my Buck Skinner Hunting Knife.

Third (and last): *The problem of polemics*. There was no way in the world that I wanted to be caught in a state of naked self-justification for what would undoubtedly be seen as an act of egregious overkill. After all, what crimes had been committed by The Seven to deserve such a judgment, and who was I to carry out that judgment with such severity ... and with such style? Well, like it or not, there are no rules in these matters – only impulses, the exercise of power, and a convenient time and place (motive, means, and opportunity in the squinty eyes of the Law).

Question: Were there no other options that might have been less violently explored?
Answer: None that presented themselves to my obsessive-compulsive brain.

Question: Couldn't I have sought professional aid to control my mania?
Answer: I had already swallowed a candy store of medications without appreciable results (except a constant cramp in my gut). And I had undergone a kaleidoscope of therapies which were not any more effective than the meds, although at least they didn't affect my digestive system.

Question (reprise): Wasn't there *some* other course of action I might have pursued?
Answer: If there had been, I would have; since I didn't, there wasn't.

So those were the matters that occupied my mind, along with a lot of other nonsense, as I made my final outing of the day to an office supply store. I would certainly need to buy plenty of paper and some extra cartridges of toner in order to bring forth an adequate declaration, an ultimate statement, of all the facts . . . my letter of resignation from the human race.

At the check-out counter my credit card finally breathed its last, and when I left the store I tossed it in the nearest trash container. Then it occurred to me that I wouldn't be needing any of the other documents I had collected in my wallet over the years, and so I tossed all of that junk away too, along with the wallet itself – that battered old pal of my back pocket. Freed of these encumbrances of official identity, I practically soared like a huge black crow through the October twilight back to my apartment.

Nonetheless, my mind was still spinning about, fretting over the precise form and phrasing of my Ultimate Statement. It seemed to me that there remained some issue that I had yet to face, some vague but fundamental question I had not regarded, some abysmal matter that I still could not approach, that possibly no human brain had ever approached.

Of course the simple answer to everything I was about to do was that I felt myself trapped in a maze of pain, and the only course of action that presented itself to my mortal faculties was to shoot my way out. I could always fall back on that as my closing line.

However, all of this mental exercise came to a skidding halt when I realized that, due to my state of distraction, I had left my goods back at the office supply store . . . and it was almost closing time. Spinning around on the sidewalk, I began racing back toward my point of purchase. But something happened that kept me from ever reaching that destination.

When it happened: I couldn't say.

Where it happened: I couldn't say.

What it was: That I could say.

It was the loudest sound I had ever heard in my life.

Part II

1

There was only darkness. It flowed like a black river that had no bottom. And it was unconfined by any shores, infinite and turbulent and moving without direction, without any source or destination. There was only darkness flowing in darkness.

Then something felt itself struggling in this black and bottomless and infinite river, something unformed and embryonic swirling within the darkness. It had no eyes, just as the darkness had none. It had no thoughts and no sensations, only the darkness flowing through it and around it in a blind chaos of thrashing agitation. It was something living, something restless and alive in the darkness that flowed relentlessly like a black river in a black world. Yet even without eyes or thoughts or sensations it moved toward the impossible surface of the darkness . . . and broke through.

I had always been afraid of the dark. Now it was all around me, a vicious and sinister presence without shape or name. And it was also inside me, so that I could not escape it by any means of flight and was paralyzed with fear. But slowly it began to withdraw – that nameless darkness, that vicious and sinister presence which is encountered only in the worst nightmares – hiding itself away once again and allowing forms to appear as if in a dull moonlight, letting in those thoughts and sensations required for the creation of a self. And as if I had been dreaming, it seemed that I had been gone forever. And as if I had been dreaming, it seemed I had been gone for no time at all.

It was night, and I was in my apartment above Lillian's diner. (How had I gotten there? Where was I before the darkness blinded my mind?) One certainty: I did not inhabit the space around me in the same way I had before. I could move throughout the rooms of my apartment, yet I did not use or need to use a human form to do so. (How could this be happening? What had been done with my body?) By force of will alone I found myself rising from the floor and floating like a cobweb in a corner of the ceiling. I could see the moonlight beaming through the old curtains of the window by my desk.

Another mystery: I could now see beyond the curtains and through the window into a dizzying maze of rooms and hallways and streets and alleys, my mind spinning in a thousand directions until I was forced to make it stop. Following this exercise, I opened my ears – just for a moment – to an incoherent choir of voices, cutting them off before I became lost in their senseless babble.

There were so many frightening things, so many questions and conundrums during this dream-like phase of an experience that I knew was no dream at all. But any answers were evasive and fled into opaque regions where my mind could not pursue them. Every time I tried to penetrate into these areas I found myself trapped in a dead-end thick with shadows, what I came to think of as 'dark spots' where that black river flowed bubbling and viscous. These dark spots were a source of both fear and frustration for me. They suggested the presence of an unknown player in a game I was only beginning to learn.

I was still my same obsessive-compulsive self – that was a further certainty – and I did not like the feeling that

schemes and strategies were being carried out around me
... that secret meetings had taken place behind my back ...
that I had been condemned for something I did not do ...
that I had been manipulated and humiliated ... that my
competence had been questioned by buffoons, my messages
ignored by morons ... that I had been railroaded into the
status of a non-person in an organization I had served so
long and so well ... and ultimately dismissed from even
that lick-spittle job.

Work not done! Work not done!

Their faces now crowded everything else from my
thoughts. It was my final wish, my very special plan, to see
those faces screaming and bloody and finally laid lifeless at
my feet – how well I recalled all of *that*. But the Monday-
morning ballistic blowout had been cancelled. In my present
state I couldn't even hold a piece of paper. (Paper, paper –
why did this word echo in my mind for a moment, only to
fade and die in the grip of those dark spots?) How then
could I wield a head-shattering USP Tactical or a knee-
capping Glock 17? I couldn't even see my own face as I
hovered before my bathroom mirror. I would never be able
to present that face as the last thing those swine would ever
see on the day of their slaughter.

And then it happened. The machinery of my murderous
rage was grinding its gears, burning its oil into toxic vapors,
shooting out sparks right and left, shooting and shooting ...
until the mirror before me began to glow with an eerie
incandescence. There it was, at the center of that infernal
aura. There was my face, radiant with obsessive hate. There
were my eyes, pitching daggers from behind amber-tinted
lenses. There I stood in the full blackness of my form. And
in my left hand was my Buck Skinner Hunting Knife. I
raised it up and pressed the side of that blade lightly against
my cheek, nearly swooning with a black joy.

After this first manifestation I let myself fade back into
the shadows. I now had the ability to control the substance
of myself. I would later learn to control the powers of my

sight and my hearing. And there were other things, forces and faculties unheard of and marvelous, that I would soon discover.

My work would not be left undone. My work was only beginning.

2

Two homicide detectives – one black, one white, both gray – got off the elevator at an old downtown office building and entered the reception area of a company that was the building's oldest and most prosperous lessee. They noted the soft lighting and expensive decor (with grand piano) but did not seem intimidated in the least. Both of them had visited the old building many times over the years.

As Detective White said to Detective Black in the elevator, 'There used to be a soda fountain on the ground floor of this place. Best hot-fudge sundaes I ever had in my life. My parents used to take me there when we lived in the city.'

'Long time ago,' commented Detective Black.

'Yup,' said Detective White with only the vaguest hint of sentimental reflection in his voice.

From the reception area they were shuttled up to the twentieth (twenty-first?) floor, where they were greeted by another receptionist slash administrative assistant who was awaiting their arrival. Marsha Linstrom, according to the brass name-plate on her desk, ushered the homicide detectives into the office of the company's CEO, who had no personal knowledge that could aid them in this police matter but who gave them carte blanche to move about the company offices with the guidance of a woman that Marsha called up from Human Resources. As they began descending the stairway that shot like a spine through the ten floors of the company's office space, Marsha Linstrom – a factotum of superior efficiency – was already on the phone instructing someone to find out the 'where and when' of the funeral and to order the customary arrangement of flowers which the company always sent on the occasion of an employee's demise.

Down in HR, the homicide detectives asked to see the company's file on the deceased, as well as the files of persons who worked closely with the deceased, along with the files of any employees who had recently left the company 'not in good standing'. Earlier that day the homicide detectives, to their satisfaction, had determined the friends and family members of the deceased to be poor suspects. An investigation at the victim's workplace was simply the next step in a fairly mechanical process. The two men each took notes based on the information provided by the employee files they examined.

'Why don't we work this Frank Dominio guy first. Talk to his supervisor,' said Detective Black.

'Yeah, I know,' replied his partner. 'His file doesn't exactly paint a picture of the ideal employee. And the stigma of a forced resignation can really irk some people.'

'Sounds like you're speaking from personal experience.'

'I say it in confidence,' said Detective White.

'A guy would have to be incredibly irked to do this thing,' said Detective Black, producing a manila envelope that he had folded up in the pocket of his overcoat.

'I guess it depends on the guy.'

But the Young Supervisor with whom the homicide detectives spoke had nothing of interest to add to Frank Dominio's dossier, not wittingly anyway. Mr Dominio hadn't worked very long in the Young Supervisor's department before he handed in his resignation. 'You should talk to someone who worked with Domino longer than I did. I've only been with the company about a year.'

'I thought his name was DoMINio,' said Detective Black.

'Didn't I say that?' replied the Young Supervisor, lying arrogantly.

'No, you said Domino,' confirmed Detective White.

'Well, I didn't mean to say that,' said the Young Supervisor, suddenly repentant. 'So what did Frank do?'

'Thank you for your time, Mr Chipmunk,' said Detective Black.

'It's Chipman.'

'My mistake.'

Then the homicide detectives turned and walked to their next, and best, subject of interrogation.

'Twelfth floor. Richard Somebody,' said Detective White, glancing at his notes.

'Mind if we make a pit stop first?'

'I was about to suggest the same thing.'

In the men's room, which was located outside of company space and still had most of the original fixtures from the time of the building's pre-Depression-era construction, the homicide detectives relieved themselves in surroundings of massive marble walls, heavy wooden doors fronting spacious toilet stalls, and deep porcelain sinks with separate handles for hot and cold water. The first to zip up, Detective Black strode over to the sink and pulled both handles toward him, cupping his hands under the single spigot. But no water came rushing into his waiting palms, only a great groaning sound that rumbled inside the walls and made the porcelain basin shake before his eyes. He backed away from the sink as his partner looked on. What ultimately emerged from the goose-necked metal spigot was a thick oily fluid, as if the lavatory's plumbing had tapped into a black river of sewage.

'It *is* an old building,' shouted Detective White over the loud rumbling inside the walls, which by now had modulated into a beastlike growl.

'Yeah,' said Detective Black as he cautiously pushed back both the hot and cold handles on the sink, bringing the room back to its former state of weighty silence.

'Come on,' said Detective White. 'We have to see a man about a murder.'

When they arrived at Richard's office it was obvious that he was expecting them. He rose from his desk and vigorously shook hands with the homicide detectives, introducing himself, and then closed the door. He invited his two visitors to seat themselves in the chairs positioned before his desk, and then returned to his own chair behind it.

'What terrible news you bring us,' Richard said. 'I can't believe it. But why wasn't there anything in the media about it?'

'The body was discovered just this morning,' explained Detective Black. 'We kept the news people out of the loop a little longer than usual on this one because the circumstances of Mr Stokowski's death were somewhat unusual.'

'Unusual? In what way?'

'From the files we examined, you were Mr Stokowski's immediate superior for a period of some years,' said Detective White. 'We were hoping that you or some of the others who worked more closely with the victim might be able to help us in a way that the others we've spoken with have not.'

'I don't understand,' said Richard.

Detective Black opened the manila envelope he'd been carrying around and pulled out some photographs, handing them across the desk to Richard. 'These are photos taken at the crime scene. What they reveal has not been made known to the media.'

Richard leafed through the photographs without any change of facial expression, which must have been difficult even for him, considering the images now passing before his eyes. Detective Black placed these images in context for the benefit of Mr Stokowski's former boss.

'Mr Stokowski's car was found by two officers patrolling the area around the abandoned warehouse you see in the photos. Considering that it was a relatively expensive vehicle and in good condition, they phoned in the license tags to see if it had been reported as stolen.'

'And had it?' asked Richard.

'No,' answered Detective White, picking up the narrative. 'The officers then investigated the warehouse. Almost immediately they came across the victim tied to an old office chair and pushed up against that wall in the pictures.'

'It looks like there's something wrong with his hands,' said Richard.

'They're not hands,' said Detective White. 'Well, they're not real hands. They're from a mannikin – two left hands. Somebody very strong cut off Mr Stokowski's hands – we're still looking for those – and somehow fused the ends of his wrists to those, uh, artificial hands.'

'It's fairly obvious that the killer wasn't trying to hide his work,' said Detective Black. 'He very much wanted the body to be found in that condition and on that exact spot – undisturbed. Do you see the writing on the wall just above the victim's head?'

'Yes,' said Richard.

'The letters,' said Detective White, 'seem to have been burned right into the wall, possibly with an acetylene torch. Can you see what it says?'

'It looks like "Work" or "Word". "Word Note Gone?"' said Richard.

'WORK NOT DONE,' corrected Detective Black. 'All capital letters. It's written very clearly if you look close.'

'All right, I see it now,' admitted Richard. 'But I still don't understand why you would think that I might be able to shed any light on this . . . atrocity.'

'We were hoping that the words, the hands, anything you see here, might mean something to you,' said Detective White. ' "Work Not Done" seems a natural enough phrase to be used in one's workplace. Or maybe you recognize the handwriting, although I know that's a long shot.'

'It surely is. Everything written in all caps looks the same to me,' said Richard as he arranged the photos into a neat pile and placed them on his desk at a distance from himself. 'No, I'm sorry – none of it means anything to me.'

'Well, perhaps you could bring this up – as discreetly as possible – with some of Mr Stokowski's coworkers,' said one of the homicide detectives as they got up from their seats. 'See if they can think of something. Just the part about the writing, you understand. We'd like to keep the rest of it out of the media as long as we can.'

Detective Black then collected the photographs and replaced them in the manila envelope. Detective White left a card on Richard's desk with a phone number and a – gack! – email address where the homicide detectives could be reached. Richard began to open the door for the two men, but then pushed it closed again.

'If I might ask,' Richard said. 'You never specified what was the cause of death. I suppose it was the hands. The trauma, the bleeding.'

Detective White smiled and said, 'The verdict's not in on that one. Most likely it was the hands.'

'Most likely,' repeated Detective Black.

Then, for just a moment, Richard became as still as stone. He knew they were lying to him, but all he could do was express his sincere hope that they would soon apprehend the killer, adding, almost in a whisper, 'Perry was a very well-liked employee at this company.'

'I'm sure he was,' said Detective Black, who then casually flipped through a few pages in his notebook. Then, almost as an afterthought, he said, 'And this Domino guy – I gather that he wasn't one of the most popular people around here.'

'Excuse me?' said Richard the Innocent.

'Frank Dominio,' said Detective White, just to clarify the identity of the employee in question.

'Oh, yes,' responded Richard without a hint of commitment to any knowledge regarding Mr Dominio.

'We understand that he wasn't exactly a model employee,' said Detective Black. 'Mr Chipman said that you were the person to talk to about this guy. He resigned from the company yesterday?'

'I didn't know that,' said Richard. 'Well, as you already seem to know, he wasn't the sort who was going to be named employee of the month. It's true that he worked under me for some time, but . . . you know how it is. Some people don't make much of an impression on you. And I've seen so many come and go.'

'So Mr Dominio was just another guy who went,' said Detective Black.

'As far as I know,' said my old boss.

Now it was Richard's turn to see his interrogators turn into rock-solid doubters of his word. So how did it feel, Richard – to be left standing there as Detectives White and Black left your office knowing – *knowing* – that you had lied to them? Lied, Richard, and not to just some-body around the office, but to a couple of homicide detectives.

How well you must have known that they knew there was something wrong about you. So how did it feel?

3

I had always been easily moved to feel affection or admiration for people whom I viewed only from afar. And this is how I felt toward Detectives White and Black as I spied on them from the remote observatory of my apartment, tuning in their voices and images on my personal airwaves, keeping myself at a spectral distance from the eyes and ears of these law enforcement veterans. They seemed very good at what they did, very dedicated and phlegmatic in a way that suited men of their age who had seen the things they must have seen in their professional lives – the corpse of Perry Stokowski for instance – and who knew what to say and what not to say to the people, or swine, they were forced to deal with on a daily basis. I almost felt guilty that they had no hope of achieving a successful conclusion to the case they were presently working.

But how I appreciated Detective White's memory of those hot-fudge sundaes he had enjoyed in the building where I once worked, not to mention the way Detective Black handled Supervisor Chipman when that little crumb knowingly corrupted my surname. But that one little word, Domino, wasn't going to help those admirable and affection-worthy homicide detectives. They would still be looking at it from a thousand angles when they ultimately declared the case, still in its infancy, unsolved.

And best of all was Richard's stony look of visibly repressed frustration when Detectives White and Black had so transparently lied to him in claiming that the cause of Mr Stokowski's death was unknown at the present time. I thought I even saw a genuine flinch of fear in Richard's face. (As sweet to me as one of those hot-fudge sundaes of Detective White's childhood.) Of course it would not have been possible, and certainly not desirable, to reveal the bizarre truth of this aspect of the case. Then they would really be taken for liars, or possibly lunatics.

In the photos they had shown Richard, Perry's head was slumped crookedly downward in fine corpse-like fashion. Anyone could see that he was still wearing his eyeglasses, I made sure of that. But what couldn't be seen was that the red-tinted lenses were almost entirely gone. Little trace of them was found at the crime scene – only a broken sliver of the left lens that remained in those thick black frames. It wasn't until an autopsy had been performed, a show that I attended 'in person', that the coroner found the pulverized pieces of Perry's lenses jaggedly embedded throughout the cadaver's system. The redly tinted shrapnel had torn up the victim's veins and arteries, were jammed jaggedly into the inner walls of his intestines, and had collected into a tough little cluster – like a glass raspberry – in his aorta. 'I don't get it. How did this stuff get in here?' queried the coroner. 'It's as if someone injected it into his system.'

Close enough, doctor. I deliberately left that sliver of red lens in Perry's glasses so that the comparison could be made with the splinters that flowed along the red river inside him and ripped him apart from within. Red goes into red. It made sense to me. Then again, I was insane, a monster, an inhuman malefactor with no good excuse for its abominable actions.

One would think, as you are probably thinking, that someone who was no longer among the living might have risen above his earthly rage, might have gained enough perspective to withdraw from the petty games that had once pinned his body to the world. But there was really no way to be sure that in fact I was no longer among the living. Even though I did not 'live' in the usual sense of the word – example: I no longer suffered from bodily needs such as hunger, thirst, or sleep – there remained a definite material aspect to my existence.

Perry certainly considered me a physical threat when he first saw me in the rearview mirror of his car as he drove away from the Straight Ahead jazz club that night. When I put my Buck Skinner Hunting Knife to his throat he felt the blade . . . he started begging and sniveling . . . and he heard my voice instruct him where to steer his jazzy little vehicle. And afterward I walked out of that derelict warehouse, alone, the way I had come in with Perry, which was the same entrance I had used on that day I visited the abandoned structure and discovered those mannikin hands and cartoon-character gloves. I wiped Perry's blood off the knife and onto the right leg of my black denim pants. I noted with annoyance that it was darker than it ought to have been at that hour of the morning due to the 'daylight savings' time-change.

Indeed, following my execution of Perry it appeared to be far darker than it ought to have been, even considering that hour which was annually excised for several months from the time zone I inhabited. It looked to me, as I stood in the moonlight of the empty field beside the warehouse, that there was a blackness behind the blackness of the black sky, some constellation of 'black spots', like stars in negative photographic exposure, which collected above me and which I felt only I could see. But although this blackness, in my perception, did seem to describe a kind of constellation far off in the galaxy overhead, I also sensed in the most intimate way that it was connected to that fearsome *presence* I had encountered so recently.

On the way back to my apartment this formation of dark stars, along with the fear that accompanied them, faded away to a large extent. Yet even as morning broke there still remained some residue, in my peculiar vision, of those dark spots . . . leaving a kind of stain upon the sky, a dirty smear that never entirely dissipated. No mention was made of this phenomenon by the local weather reports, which I was able to check and recheck quite thoroughly using my newly gained powers of surveillance. Somehow I knew that these dark spots of the night, these stains upon the daytime sky, were not visible to any living persons.

Yet I still did not believe myself to be dead. This conviction didn't merely derive from the fact that I had been a lifelong non-believer in an afterlife – I was always willing to concede my errors of opinion when sufficient evidence arose to the contrary. But no evidence of the kind presented itself, no matter how hard I searched for it. No newspaper obituary – those little boxes with tiny letters inside – had reported the death of Francis Vincent Dominio. My name appeared nowhere in any of the official records that I scanned in my own fashion. Thus, I had to conclude that I was *not dead*, even if I was obviously no longer among the living.

This situation might have been a great problem for me if I had not been so preoccupied with other business. I still had some special plans to make. And I also knew that it wouldn't be long before Detectives White and

Black followed up on their information concerning a bad apple who had 'hereby resign[ed] effective immediately' from the company where Mr Stokowski had until recently been employed and who, now that the homicide detectives finally noticed it, had worked closely with the deceased for a number of years.

White and Black would soon be asking Lillian about the tenant in the apartment above the Metro Diner. Before that happened, I needed to get some of my affairs in order.

4

'Hello, idiot.'

The voice was Richard's and the person addressed was Supervisor Chipman.

'What did you say to them?' Richard asked.

'Nothing,' said Chipman like a child who was trying to cover up some misdeed.

'You called him Domino.'

'So what?' said Chipman.

An expression of sly calm suddenly appeared on Richard's face. 'So what, indeed,' Richard seemed to be thinking as he eased his weight against Chipman's cubicle counter and complacently crossed his arms, cheerfully chastising himself for having overreacted. Some people are obsessive-compulsives. Richard merely had an instinct for devious caution, for hyper-vigilance in the cause of self-interested wile.

'Hey, I didn't show *this* to anybody, if that's what's worrying you.'

As Chipman spoke these words he simultaneously slid open the bottom drawer of his desk. Inside was a stack of papers on top of which was a page from a yellow legal pad that, in my handwriting, read: WORK NOT DONE.

'Oh, Christ,' said Richard, kicking the drawer closed with his huge wing-tipped foot. Then he gingerly pulled out the desk drawer just enough to slide in his fingers and remove the piece of paper with the handwriting on it, crumpling it into a little paper ball that disappeared inside his right hand just before his hand disappeared within the pin-striped pocket of his trousers. 'Now get rid of the rest of it, pinhead.'

'I didn't know I was supposed to,' said Chipman the Clueless.

'What you don't know is going to seriously affect your advancement around here. Understood?'

'Yeah,' said Chipman.

'Yeah?' mocked Richard.

'Yes, I understand.'

'Good. And no more talk about anybody called Domino.'

'Yes, I understand,' Chipman mocked back. This was somewhat unwise because now he was on Richard's list as well as on mine. I wondered who would get to him first.

5

That same afternoon, Richard called an emergency 'lunch meeting' of The Seven – excuse me, Six. I didn't exactly need this distraction at the moment, since I was scrambling against the clock (darn that lost hour!) and was forced to divide my attention between the work at hand in my apartment and the lunchtime scene at the company.

Sidebar: Anthropologists who once held that all human activity could be reduced to the three F's – Feeding, Fighting, and, in the present instance, a little Fondling – would have been pleased to see how closely their hypothesis was enacted at the banquet table in that Gothic Gallery where I used to assemble with this contemptibly familiar cast of characters and where their lunch-meeting was now in progress.

Sherry popped the lid on a plastic bowl filled with vegetables sliced up into spears. But she suddenly stopped short. 'I forgot to bring anything to drink,' whined the Sherry-thing, who was sitting close to the head of the table, immediately to Richard's left. The meal that Richard had brought along consisted only of an extra thermos of coffee. He took a swig directly from the mouth of the thermos he had already opened – a shining metal silo – and then slid it over to Sherry, who just gawked at it for a moment, as if she were looking at some exotic artifact she had never seen before.

'Here,' said Richard, slapping the plastic cap of the thermos before Sherry's eyes, which no more recognized this 'particular object than they had the other. 'You can use it as a cup,' Richard explained.

'But –' Sherry started to say.

'Yes, I know,' said Richard with fatherly wisdom and understanding. Then he reached down into Sherry's purse on the floor between them, rummaged around inside it, and came up with a miniature bottle of vodka. He casually ran his hand along Sherry's leg before bringing the dwarf-sized bottle up to her. 'Go ahead,' he said to her. 'Everybody knows.' Sherry went ahead and daintily dumped the spirits into the plastic container, then quickly dropped the evidence of her alcoholism back in her purse before pouring in the coffee, awkwardly maneuvering Richard's shining metal thermos.

Barry the Great-Bodied One removed the first of several hamburgers from a sack that sagged heavily upon that banquet table. But his eyes were fixed across the table at what Kerrie was shoveling into her mouth from a field-style plate with attached covering.

'What are you looking at, Mr America?' said Kerrie.

'I'm just trying to identify that stuff you're eating.'

'It's leftovers.'

'Right,' said Barry with a world of doubt in his voice.

Further down the table Mary sat before the cardboard dish – square and shallow – of a microwaved meal. (Swedish Meatballs and Noodles in Gravy – her favorite, although she sometimes broke up the monotony with Salisbury Steak, topped with Mushroom Sauce, and Macaroni and Cheese.)

Harry wasn't eating, waving off Barry's offer of a hamburger. 'I've got plenty,' said Barry.

'I'm sure you do, thanks,' said the inscrutable Harry.

It was also lunchtime at the Metro Diner, and the place was packed. I didn't see the homicide detectives anywhere around. However, I knew they had run a check on my credit card activity: the gun shop, the clothes store, the . . . the . . . paper? (Did I buy a newspaper that night? If so, I wouldn't have used my credit card.) But even though I couldn't bring into my brain any other spending I had done, I couldn't shake the feeling that there was something else, something far more significant than paper, that was also being masked by those dark spots. In any case, I knew that soon the cops would be beating on my door, and it was imperative that Lillian made it up to my apartment before they did. My tactic for doing this involved a baseball bat that once served as my only means of 'personal protection'. Gripping this shapely piece of wood, I stood before my computer monitor as if I were facing a hated pitcher on a rival team. I wound up my swing and –

'All right, then,' said Richard. 'As we all know by now we have a problem.'

'No kidding,' said Sherry. 'What happened? You said that Frank was finished. Instead we've got one dead Polack.'

'These things don't always go according to plan,' said Richard.

'Yeah, like that girl, Andrea What's-Her-Name, ending up dead on your desk,' said Kerrie, who continued sporking a mysterious mash into her mouth. 'You said Frank would go quietly. Now it's a mess.'

'Before you leave the room to go vomit up your lunch, Kerrie, I'd like to point out that the problem wasn't with Domino – it was with Perry Stokowski. He was the mess.'

'How so?' asked Mary.

'To put it simply, Perry wasn't quite a full member of our family.'

'Please, Richard, I've got enough with my real family at home. I don't need to think in terms of a second family.'

'That's where you're wrong, Mary,' said Richard. 'Let me ask you something. Who do you prefer spending your time with, not to mention most of your extra time – those people at home . . . or us?'

Mary looked thoughtfully down at the empty microwave-proof container on the table before her.

'You can't lie to me, Mary. Or to the rest of us. We are your family. *We* are the only family that any of us have. Oh, some of you may have spouses or someone you live with, even children. But they aren't your family. Why do you think you're sitting at this table with us? It wasn't by chance, I can tell you. It's because I *chose* you.'

I had to call time-out back at my apartment because I had forgotten to unplug my computer. My purpose wasn't to start a fire in that old building but to get Lillian's attention. (And no, Kerrie, I would not be going quietly – I would go with quite a bit of noise and mayhem.) After I had dealt with the potential threat of an electrical fire, I finally swung my bat. Disappointingly, it made only a spider-web pattern of cracks in the computer screen. (Downstairs in the diner, amidst all the lunch-hour chewing and chattering, my first hit went unnoticed. Strike one.) My next swing was dedicated to Andrea and the others who had been done in by Richard. I connected well with the monitor and sent it into the farthest bleachers, where Richard sat sipping coffee from a thermos on a sunny afternoon. In short order the monitor was just a pile of glass and plastic lying on the floor. Beside it was the keyboard whose teeth I then smashed with a lusty surge of madness. A momentary hiatus of conversation ensued in the diner below, as well as a suspension of service on the part of Rudy and the waitresses. And Lillian at last glanced upward toward my apartment.

'You may have hired all of us, Richard. But that includes Perry,' argued Mary. 'You said yourself that he wasn't a member of this family of yours.'

'I said he wasn't a *full* member. I thought he would have become so in time. But I didn't think it would take so long to wean him off that music nonsense on which he wasted so much of himself. He wasn't fully focused on the one important thing in all our lives – The Job. That caused him to let his guard down. Now he's gone, rest in peace.'

'Excuse me, Richard, but none of what you're saying accounts for Frank Dominio. If there was ever someone who wasn't one of us, it was Frank. Why in the world did you "choose" him?'

'Frank?' said Richard. 'He was one of the family too . . . in a red-headed stepchild capacity. The truth is we really needed Frank. Please don't take this personally, any of you. That is, each of you has your uses. Otherwise you wouldn't be here. But Frank had something the rest of you don't, including myself. It was just a matter of time before he brought it to us. None of us could have come up with that.'

'You mean that idea of his?' said Sherry.

'That's right.'

'What was so great about that?' Sherry continued to badger. 'You told us to give it the cold shoulder. It seemed to me that was exactly what it deserved.'

'Barry,' said Richard, turning to his right. 'Would you enlighten her?'

Barry swallowed a cheek-stretching mouthful of macerated bread and meat, with extra-extra ketchup. Then he held up the remains of the object in his hand.

'Do you know what this is, Sherry?'

'Yeah – it's a hamburger, or what's left of one.'

'It's also Frank's idea. But even he didn't realize that. Here's the analogy. It wasn't so long ago that some stroke of genius caused the creation of these ground slabs of beef and fat inserted between two pillowy pieces of bread. Of course it was only some time later that the full lucrative potential of this edible invention was realized. Could any of us have invented the hamburger? Not likely.'

Sherry suddenly smiled, a mouthful of coffee and vodka almost spilling forth. 'But we would sure know how to market the things,' she practically cried out.

'Billions and billions of them,' added Kerrie.

Swine, swine, swine, etc. Each utterance of this word was accompanied by a smashing blow upon the metal box of my modem. Then I dropped my bat, abandoning this primitive means of destruction, and went to work on the beast's entrails in the fashion of my new-born self – tying the transistors into the tiniest knots with only a twitch of my mind, melting wiring boards and decimating the soul of that thing – those diabolical chips – on an atomic level. Nobody was going to get into my mind through that infernal machine. And you, Richard – you knew, you *knew* my idea was brilliant, that I was worth more than all the rest of you. But you let me contort myself into a mass of obsessive doubt and self-loathing. Laugh while you can, you swine.

Mary was in fact tittering at her end of the table, while Richard was outright guffawing in a deep dark tone. Even Harry cracked a crooked grin. It was so nice to see such a happy family. But the magic moment died when Kerrie spoke up, hesitantly asking, 'But wasn't there a lot more documentation to Frank's idea? Don't we need that?'

'We'll see. Maybe we do and maybe we don't. We do want to cover all the bases, don't we, Harry?'

'Yes, sir,' Harry replied. Everyone else grew quiet.

'Do you think you can work as well without Perry's assistance?'

'It'll be better without him,' said Harry. 'It was because of him that the Andrea What's-Her-Name thing went badly. I never said anything.'

'I know,' said Richard. 'I didn't blame you.'

'He was a worthless drug addict,' said Harry. (As an addendum to Harry's remark, I should mention that it was Perry's syringe in his glove compartment that gave me the idea for the intravenous mode of his murder.) After Harry had finally gotten that bit of bile out of himself about Perry's dope fiendery, he looked over at Sherry and said, 'No offense.'

The eyes of the Sherry-thing glared at Harry. 'It's not the same thing,' she hissed. 'My name is Sherry. *And I am an alcoholic!* Got it?'

'Uh, yeah,' said Harry, who obviously couldn't have cared less one way or the other.

Lillian was finally knocking on my door and calling out my name. I had left the door slightly ajar, causing it to push open easily and allowing Lillian to exercise her landlord's privilege to investigate what all the noise was about in her tenant's apartment. Cautiously she entered the kitchen through the backstairs door. By the time Lillian was inside I had absented myself from visibility. The last thing I wanted was to put a scare into the only person who came close to being family to me. (You were right to a certain extent, Richard – I was as alienated as the rest of you from my own blood relations.)

Lillian did draw a startled breath when she first spied the mutilated machine lying about my apartment floor. I had pushed most of the pieces aside, creating a path to lead her straight to my desk and the shoe box that was waiting there for her. She picked up the box and mouthed the words written on its lid that addressed the package to her. She then reached under the apron she was wearing and from within her waitress's uniform produced a pocketknife. It was no Buck Skinner Hunting Knife but a business-like instrument nonetheless. Good for you, Lil, I thought. After pulling the blade from its slot, she cut the packing tape wrapped around the shoe box, lifted off the top, and gazed upon the stack of packets which constituted the whole of my worldly worth. 'My god,' she gasped. Quickly putting two and two together, she said aloud, 'I guess this means I won't be seeing you any more, Frank. Good luck to you.' Lillian looked so sad as she replaced the lid back on the box and cradled the package under her arm.

Before leaving my apartment, locking the door behind her with her landlord's key ('Thank you, Lillian Hayes'), she turned for a moment to look around the place. She could not possibly have seen me as I watched her from my niche of the non-living. But somehow she fixed her eyes, if briefly, on the exact spot where I was looking back at her. Then she was gone, and I shifted my visual and auditory attention back to the gathering in the Great Hall.

'One more thing,' said Mary. 'I assume we're not doing this just so the company can make a pile out of it and leave us with, at most, some miserable little "bonus"?'

'As the head of this family I must withhold from you, for your own good, mind you, the full details of this venture. For now let me just say that things are going to get a little rickety around here once Barry's plan for restructuring the company is put in place – all of this having been done, of course, at the behest of the CEO and seconded by all of senior management. There just may be a period of declining profits visited on this house due to a chaotic work environment. Soon the stockholders will begin making sounds of discontent and start pawing the ground like a herd of unfed cattle looking for some new cowboys to run the ranch – people with fresh ideas and special plans. Before you know it . . . *we* will be the company.'

But one thing at a time, they agreed.

First things first, they agreed.

And that first thing was Domino, who could queer this whole business if they didn't get to him before the cops did.

That was your cue, Harry. And I'd be keeping a special eye on you.

6

I have to confess that I was as much relieved as I was enraged by the revelations of infamy that the lunch-meeting of The Six had afforded my long-distance eyes and ears. Not that they proved themselves to be any more swinish than I had imagined them to be. They couldn't possibly have done that. But my image of them had always been that of a pack of beasts whose deeds were performed somewhat haphazardly, directed by a low animal instinct that sniffed out creatures who were not of their breed and marked them for a mindless savaging. Given this conception of their brutish nature, I was naturally driven to respond in kind with plans for a very basic style of massacre, although one for which I had accessorized myself to the hilt with all the appropriate gear and suitably dark attire. Therefore, what a surprise – at once disturbing and delightful – to discover how well these beings knew what they were about.

Disturbing because they had schemes and strategies and an ambitious end in sight. They had turned out to be a tribe of true fiends, a devilish cabal, a Machiavellian mob with Richard as The Prince who commanded a court of hench-persons.

Delightful for the very same reasons. I found it so satisfying to have my worst suspicions about The Six, formerly Seven, finally, unequivocally confirmed. They were indeed a bad lot. My murder-filled mind – driven by an obsessive-compulsive engine of emotion which the nonafflicted cannot hope to comprehend, spinning itself on a carousel of Fear, Hate, Humiliation, and divers other riderless horses of my personal apocalypse – had *not* gone too far in its violent fantasies.

Yet fantasies were all they amounted to. Even when I began making preparations to behave in accordance with my raging impulses, which, I concede, were a bit overblown for having been planted so deeply within me and suppressed far too long – the situation was still at the stage of daydreams and play-acting. And the Day of Domino was destined never to arrive – not as I had originally conceived it as a bullet-fest on Monday morning. (Who can say if I would actually have gone through with it?) That day had not only been pushed back (due to circumstances beyond my control and still obscure to my mind, however much I sought them out); it had also been drastically altered in its possibilities.

Let's step back for a moment. Frank Dominio was a man of hyper-charged and off-kilter imagination, no denying it; but he had always been held back by his fears and inner demons. Domino, on the other hand, was not only completely warped, he also belonged to a class of demon himself. Both of them did share many like qualities. Among these was an eagerness to get started on a project, if only to put it behind them as soon as possible. Thus, my work, our work, was not deferred until Monday but began as Wednesday passed into Thursday (EDT). And short work it was that we, 'I' for the sake of convenience, made of Mr Stokowski.

I giggled like a child on Christmas morning as I tackled each task with respect to Perry the Piano Player, Perry the Jazz-Creep (big deal if his penchant for music was deep and genuine, rather than the put-on I took it to be), and, as Harry called him, Perry the Worthless Drug Addict. The whole business of that night was, for me, therapeutic in a way that none of the pills or psychiatric services I had consumed over the years had ever been.

And that was exactly the problem: I was so satiated by the job I had done on Perry Stokowski that I feared I might lack the Will to follow through with the others on my gun-shop shopping list. So where would that have left me? What becomes of an ontological anomaly – that is, my own miracle-working self – when he begins to feel that his WORK, in fact, IS DONE? The dark constellations spread across the sky during the final hours of that night, along with the sooty stains that appeared when the sun rose, an hour late, the following day, did not strike me as happy portents of what lay in store for me once I had played out my purposes in the, so to speak, grand scheme of things.

Hence my relief – and double-hence my delight – at having my sheer ferocity of Will renewed by the Gang of Six at their truly revelatory lunch-meeting on Thursday afternoon. The game would now go on, and my salvation, at least for a time, was assured.

The only consternation that remained had nothing to do with Richard's foul family, with their degeneracies and devices, their sleazy comic-strip machinations, their hideous façades which hid faces that could not be countenanced. No, that was not the problem. The only source of shock left to me was that of my own lingering innocence and naiveté, the fondness I had for keeping my hot head in the cool sand. I had not given those swine nearly enough credit . . . and my credit card could not have ordered nearly enough firepower to obliterate the things that transpired in their closed-door sessions, not to mention the ever-hatching horrors which such meetings were designed to propagate, the monstrous things that popped up and hopped about, just waiting for those doors to open onto the world. This sort of thing had been going on since doors were invented . . . and they happened everywhere and at all times since the first hominids got together to 'take a meeting'.

Generally speaking: Expect nothing but nightmarish obscenities to be born when human heads come together in intercourse.

More generally speaking: Whatever is born will ultimately grow into a nightmarish obscenity – in the grand scheme of things.

Speaking for myself: There are no angels unless they are Angels of Death ... and I would never again doubt my place among them or lose my resolve to serve in their wild ranks.

7

In order to function with any effectiveness in the world, you – and that includes you – are forced to make a number of absurd assumptions. Chief among these is the assumption that yours is a reasonably sound mind in a more or less sound body moving within a rock-solid reality. Even an alcoholic like Sherry Mercer could account for any glitches that occurred in her psycho-sensory apparatus by blaming it on the booze, something she had handled relatively well in the past and had every reason to expect she could handle just as well for many years to come. This situation had begun to change for her not long after the lunch-meeting, which was the last time she would ever know anything resembling mental or metaphysical stability.

'Is everything okay, Sherry?' said one of her female staff as they were talking over some minor matters in Sherry's office.

'Everything's fine,' Sherry replied. 'But maybe we could finish this up tomorrow morning if you don't mind.'

'No problem,' said the young woman as she got up from her chair. Sherry opened the door and showed her out of the office. Then she closed the door once again, her hand trembling as it held tight to the inside door knob.

Thanks to Barry's restructuring of the company, Sherry was assigned a newly created position that came with a small private office. Previously this was a luxury and a convenience, enabling her to consume whatever quantity of alcohol she desired throughout the day and to do so in quietly dignified surroundings. Henceforth, however, that office might as well have been located deep in the heart of Hell (medieval, not modern, in the scheme of its decor).

After Sherry had closed the office door she closed her eyes. Then she haltingly turned her head toward that part of the wall which had been momentarily concealed when she opened the door. Sherry's eyelashes slowly parted, and her gaze was now directly fixed upon a place where the wall met the floor of her office.

There it was again. There it was still. It hadn't gone away, as Sherry had hoped it would.

During their meeting, she had successfully drawn the young woman's attention to that particular section of the wall. ('Is that a bug or something over there?' said Sherry, pointing right at the spot.) But she hadn't seemed to notice anything unusual within that space. Of course neither had Sherry seen anything there until a few hours ago.

But there it was again.

Behind Sherry's office door was another door. It was small and dark and ugly, a dwarf-sized portal that bulged from the wall like a scab. Its surface was coarse and irregular, as if it had been molded out of clay rather than cut from wood. Nonetheless, there did appear to be an intricate grain running through it, swirling into the door's many grooves and gouges, curling into roughly circular knots. Sherry tried not to look too closely at the dense patterns of the door, in which she had already seen a variety of little faces and parts of faces, each of them as twisted and ugly as the door itself. But this time she did squat down so that she was at eye-level with the upper edge of the door, bringing herself nearer to the thing than she had previously dared to go. Then, as though attempting to verify the nature of this phenomenon – whether actual or hallucinatory – she poised a pointy-nailed finger very close to it, ready to make a few quick taps. That was when the trouble started. Because as soon as she made contact with the door . . . her fingernail became stuck there, caught like a fly in what seemed to be a kind of tight-knit webbing rather than wood or even clay. As she pulled to extricate herself from the grasp of the door, she found that her finger sunk only more deeply into it and was soon trapped up to the cuticle.

Of course she might have called for any number of people who sat in the cubicles outside her office . . . and maybe that would have made things all right for her once more. (She had no way of knowing otherwise.) However, being the Sherry-thing that she was, she wouldn't want to be seen in her presently ridiculous – perhaps even certifiably deranged – posture. She was now seated on the floor, her short shirt riding up her rear end as she struggled to free herself, her fingertip stuck in something that no one else could see. Then –

Knock-knock-knock.

But the knocking wasn't for Sherry, it was for me. Detectives White and Black were standing outside the door that led to the backstairs of my apartment. Through the parted curtains on the door's window I stared out at the two men, who looked right through me, peering as far as they could inside. Perhaps they had a warrant to search the place for my Buck Skinner Hunting Knife, which, depending on the judge they petitioned, might be considered as the deadly tool used to sever the hands of Perry Stokowski. I hadn't been following very closely the activities of these workman-like sleuths, so I didn't know what to expect.

In any case, I thought that even if they did bust into my apartment, with or without a warrant, they wouldn't have found the knife, because somehow I had taken it with me when I entered into that spooky state of being I now enjoyed: it only took solid form when I did, and, like my black clothes and amber-tinted eyeglasses, it dissolved into thin air or moved through solid objects whenever it suited me to do so. What could be more silly than a set of clothes walking around with a pair of eyeglasses hovering over them? Or an unheld knife with a thirteen-inch blade floating down the street? So I was ready for anything the homicide detectives might have had in mind, which was something beyond my powers to know. Whatever miraculous feats I was able to perform, I still seemed to be bound by certain rules, just like anything else in this stinking world, be it animal, vegetable, mineral, vapor-form, human, superhuman, or whatever else – with all your imagination – you might be able to conceive. Everything that exists is subject to limitations imposed upon it by forces within and forces without. There are no exceptions or exemptions, although there may be some striking transformations.

Just witness what my bulked-up being was now able to do with Sherry, whose finger was sinking deeper and deeper into that ugly door. It was all my idea, my plan – at least to the extent that anyone can lay claim to an idea or plan as his very own. But how did I know I could do it? I had never done such a thing before. My original intent, way back when, was to send a bullet or two from the barrel of my Glock 17, or perhaps my Firestar, into the brain of a hated enemy, someone who had conspired to drop me into the deep end of a hell from which I did not have the power to drag myself out.

By what power, though, would my finger have pulled the trigger of that Glock, or Firestar? I knew that my Brain would ultimately give the command to shoot, shouting out, in so many words, 'OK, Finger – ready, set, fire.' But I also knew that my Brain took its orders from my Body, while at the same time functioning as an integrated part of my Body. In addition, both my Body and my Brain (as an integrated part of my Body) were reacting to pressures placed upon them by other Bodies and other Brains, such as that of Sherry in her capacity as an individual Body-Brain unit, or those of The Seven acting as a group of Bodies and Brains . . . not to mention the sundry other pressures exerted by objects and events that were without a human Body or a human Brain, including the weather, Daylight Savings Time, insects – the entire nonhuman world in general.

So how was it that all these Bodies and Brains, including my own, along with countless other nonhuman factors, such as the cockroaches that infested my apartment, could all coordinate in order to force my finger to pull the trigger of a Glock, or a Firestar, and pump some fragments of metal into Sherry Mercer's worthless Brain and well-formed Body? How could this task, or any other in this crying-shame of a world, ever be accomplished? What *precisely* was the chain of command – the source of this whole mess, the line of historical phenomena which along the way included my overwhelming urge to purchase a selection of handguns and a Buck Skinner Hunting Knife, and then later inspired me with the notion of creating this ugly little door which only Sherry, and of course I, could see . . . and that Sherry was now stuck in up to her slender wrist?

Answer: No answer, obviously.
Question: Withdrawn at the request of my dizzied Brain.

Orders to the Troops: Keep focused and continue the assault until all traces of the Sherry-pain, like that of the Perry-pain, had been neutralized.

And now the ugly little doorknob on that ugly little door began to jiggle back and forth, squeaking in Sherry's ears. It was shaped something like the head of a small monkey, but Sherry grabbed the knob without flinching, her fear of what might be trying to come through the door overcoming the loathsome look and weblike feel of all those whorls and knotholes, those little faces and parts of faces. She tried to use her hold on the knob as leverage to pull her other hand free. With this action, unfortunately, she only sank deeper into the thing, which worked in the same manner as a mind trapped in a web of obsessive thoughts: the more that you

– and definitely me – struggled to pry loose, the more tightly we would be held.

By now Sherry could feel the knob-thing pulsing with a squirmy sort of life in her one hand, while her other was lost in a place where it was being caressed by something nameless, which nevertheless might still be described as a wriggling darkness, a black world of worms slithering around her hand and between her fingers. Her eyes had opened so very wide – those Sherry-thing eyes. And now her mouth, which had once talked so much Sherry-thing talk, tried to scream. But no sound came out of that mouth. There were also other effects worked upon Sherry's body and brain, but it's better that some things be carried out behind closed doors . . . and my attention was being called elsewhere.

Apparently the homicide detectives had indeed been unable to secure a warrant to search my apartment. Detective White did rattle my doorknob rather vigorously in hopes that the wormeaten wood around the lock might give way and allow him and his partner illegal access to the suspect's residence. If I hadn't been otherwise occupied, I would have allowed them entry, purely out of politeness. Instead, the detectives had to march back down the stairs behind the diner and were now in the process of interviewing Lillian across her counter.

The place was all but empty of customers, with the exception of Harry, who was sipping coffee at the other end of the counter from Lillian and the homicide detectives.

'I do wish I could help you,' said Lillian softly. 'But I feel I must respect the privacy of my tenant.'

'We could come back with a warrant,' said Detective Black.

'That would be another matter,' said Lillian.

As the detectives continued to question Lillian, Harry was now mumbling into his cell phone out of anyone's earshot . . . except my own.

'Yeah, she's the landlord,' Harry, head down, said to Richard on the other end of the line, or rather the frequency, to Harry's phone.

'What is she saying?' said Richard.

'It's what she's *not* saying. She's lying her head off to the cops, that much I can tell.'

Detective White was trying to conceal his exasperation with the soft-spoken and flawlessly evasive responses of the diner's proprietor.

'So when was the last time you saw him?' he asked.

'I couldn't say,' said Lillian.

'Does he ever come into the diner?' asked Detective Black.

'Sometimes he does.'

Harry was able to tell that Lillian was lying to the homicide detectives because he himself must have done the same thing over and again during his career, as I inferred from my intrusions into the files of various agencies of law enforcement. Previous to Richard's hiring him ('scouting' would be a more apt term), the man I once regarded as Harry the Enigma was also known as Hank the Plumber, Joe the Roofer, and Bob the Encyclopedia Salesman, among other aliases he used for both profit (home invasion, confidence artistry; five prison years served over the course of ten life years) and pleasure (several charges of molestation involving minors, majors, and some truly aged persons when he worked as Ken the Orderly at a nursing home; no convictions).

'She's very good,' said Harry to Richard. 'I'm fairly sure she could tell us something.'

'Then find out what that something might be,' said Richard.

'It might be messy,' warned Harry.

'So be it. Messy is fine. It's sloppy I don't need.'

All right, then, Richard the Ringleader!

* * *

The homicide detectives now seemed absolutely stymied by the fact that this old woman in a waitress's uniform was getting the best of them.

'How did he seem to you when you last saw him?' asked Detective White.

'I already said that I couldn't say when I last saw him,' said Lillian.

'Does he usually come home at a particular time?' asked Detective Black.

'Maybe he does, I don't know. I really don't follow his comings and goings. I've got a business to run.'

'Did you know that he was recently forced to resign from his job?' asked Detective White.

'That wouldn't be any of my business,' said Lillian.

Having been subjected long enough to Lillian's dazzling song-and-dance, which almost moved me to tears of thanks for her protectiveness in my favor, the detectives left their card and then left the diner with two coffees to go, compliments of the house. Soon afterward Harry paid for his coffee and took his leave, only to return a few hours later as Lillian was locking up for the day.

Before Lillian had turned the key in the door, Harry came up behind her.

Before Harry came up behind her, I stepped into Lillian's body and took over its workings, placing her mind in a state of pleasant unconsciousness while I went about my business. This was another new idea of mine that came to me on the spur of the moment. I had no special plan except to keep Lillian safe. I would just have to play the rest of it by ear, and when it was over, assuming all went well, send Lillian on her way home without any alarm in her heart or memories in her head.

'Please move back inside, Ma'am,' said Harry, shoving a gun barrel into Lillian's back and nearly causing her to drop the brown carry-out bag she was juggling along with her purse while she was locking up. 'And I'll take those keys if it's all the same to you.'

Lillian had securely folded and stapled the carry-out bag, so Harry couldn't have guessed that it contained the life savings of Frank Dominio. As he maneuvered her away from the front window, Lillian said (or rather *I* said using Lillian's vocal cords), 'What is it you want, young man?'

Harry smiled at the casual tone of the question. 'I would like to rape and rob you,' he replied.

'Anything else?'

'Yes. I would like your key to the apartment upstairs. I assume you have one.'

'I surely do,' said Lillian. 'Would you mind if I set these things down on the counter?'

'Not at all.'

'Thank you. Now you said you wanted to rob me. Let me see how much I've got in my handbag.'

'Cut it out,' Harry yelled as he knocked Lillian's purse to the other side of the counter.

'No reason to act so rude,' said Lillian. 'Just a joke. I know you're not looking for some small change from this old handbag. I can see you're not just some *worthless drug addict*. Not like some people.'

Immediately Harry's attention became divided between the words he had used earlier that day to describe Perry Stokowski and the business of the moment. For a second he froze into the pose of a classic, gun-pointing hood, not even noticing that Lillian had already turned away and was headed down a hallway into the shadows of the closed diner.

'What you're looking for,' she called out from the darkness. 'It's back here.'

'Hold it,' shouted Harry.

'You hold it,' said Lillian as she opened a creaky door and switched on a light, causing a little room to appear at the end of the hallway.

When Harry entered the little room he saw Lillian standing in the corner and leaning over an old safe that opened from the top. After tuning in the combination she pulled at a metal handle and exposed the contents of the safe. 'Lots of money in here, boy,' she said. 'I was going to bring it to the bank tomorrow, just like I do every Friday.'

'Take it out,' Harry ordered.

'What do you think I'm doing?' said Lillian. After she had brought out the heavy cloth bag that contained the cash taken in at the diner, Lillian reached into the depths of the old safe and pulled up something else. 'I imagine you'd be interested in this too,' she said as she held out a stack of papers secured by a single rubber band. Harry read the words printed on the first page: 'New Product', and below these – 'Frank Dominio'.

'I knew you were lying to those cops,' Harry said in a self-satisfied voice.

'And aren't you the smart boy for taking note of that. It's too bad, though, that you won't be able to walk away with any of this loot, never mind the papers.'

'What's stopping me?' said Harry.

'Well, for one thing,' said Lillian, 'you can't open that door.'

Harry quickly turned around and realized that the door which had creaked open so loudly had somehow closed behind him without making a sound. When he swiveled back toward Lillian, she said, 'And for another thing, your gun won't work any more.'

Harry pulled the trigger of his weapon (not a Glock). But the only thing that emerged from it was a molten blob of metal, which trickled out of the cylindrical barrel like water dripping from a leaky faucet. Then the light bulb in the ceiling began to fade until the room was submerged in blackness.

These were strange phenomena in their own right. But the thing that really unsettled Harry was the sound of something bubbling up from inside the safe, illuminating the room with strangely jittering colors as it rose to the rim and emitted a vaporous stench. Harry gagged and covered his mouth with his free hand. Speaking through his fingers, he said, 'What's going on? What is that?'

'Soup of the day, boy – Cream of Mucous Membrane. I thought it might be something you'd like, you being a sexual offender and all. It does smell some.'

Harry was now choking and gagging at the same time. Finally he managed to cough out a few words. 'Who are you?' he said.

It was Lillian who looked into Harry's eyes, a lurid rainbow of glowing colors playing across her face, her mouth grinning wide. But it was my voice that answered Harry's question.

'It's me, Harry,' I said. 'It's Domino.'

I could have gone on gloating like that for some time if Harry's cell phone hadn't started chirping inside his coat pocket. This forced me to rush things, since I wanted to take that call. With lightning speed that surprised even me, I had the phone in my – that is, Lillian's – hand. By the time it was between its second and third rings, Harry was gone. The skin of his face was still bobbing up and down in the soup as it receded down into the darkness whence it came. The light in the little room switched back on.

I flipped open Harry's phone and put it to my ear. 'Hoy-hoy,' I said, continuing to speak in my own voice.

'What?' said the man on the other end, who was Richard.

'I said "Hoy-hoy". That's the phrase first put forth by Alexander Graham Bell as the standard greeting to be spoken into his new invention. Well, it wasn't just *his* invention . . . but he ended up getting all the credit for it in the public mind. That's the old story, isn't it? Especially when we – meaning you and me – are talking about brilliant and profitable inventions.'

'Is that what we're talking about?'

'You *know* that it is.'

'Where's Harry?' said Richard.

'Work not done,' I replied.

'I see,' said Richard. 'What happened exactly?'

'Sorry, Richard, but I really can't say myself what happened . . . exactly. Nothing that Harry enjoyed very much, I'm pretty sure on that score. And while we're on the subject, you might want to look in on Sherry.'

'I'll do that,' said Richard.

As I stated earlier, in order to function with any effectiveness in this world you have to make some absurd assumptions. My assumption of the moment was that Richard should have sounded far more rattled by our conversation. But this wasn't the case at all.

'That's three guys out,' I said, making the mistake of trying to get a rise out of my one-time boss. 'Four to go, not counting Chipman.'

'You're really a very bad man,' said Richard.

'Yes, I am,' I said. 'But you can take the credit for that.'

'That's no more than false modesty coming from someone with such an enormous ego. Too bad you never recognized that in yourself. We could have worked very well together if you had. It must be quite painful to have such big plans without being able to admit what an ambitious swine you really are.'

'Swine?' I said, my composure continuing to crack. I had never shared that epithet with anyone at the company.

'Isn't that what you thought of the rest of us?'

'More or less. It's a common term of derogation.'

'I suppose it is. I must have heard it used around the office. Or maybe I just dreamed it. I believe that dreams can be quite helpful in our lives. How about you?'

I was beginning to regret having answered Harry's phone. 'I think we've said about all we have to say to each other. Unless there's something you'd like to add.'

'Like what?' said Richard.

'I don't know. Something threatening. Like telling me I'm a dead man, for instance.'

'No, not at all,' said Richard. 'As far as that goes, I already *know* that you're not a dead man. But neither are you alive, isn't that right, Domino?'

Then Richard hung up, leaving me once again with a mind that was racing with incalculable doubts and questions and, above all, fear.

8

On Richard's orders, Chipman went to see what was what with Sherry. It was just after the close of the work day and the floor on which Sherry's office was located was quiet and empty, save for a few members of the cleaning staff who moved among the cubicles, emptying out each employee's trash containers and doing a bit of vacuuming. Knocking lightly on the door of Sherry's office, Chipman looked around for anyone who might be observing him before slipping into the room and closing himself inside.

'What the hell,' said Chipman aloud.

The ceiling light still illuminated the windowless office, but it was dim and flickered at strobe-like intervals. This was done strictly for effect on my part, as was the general disarray of the room, which appeared as if a miniature whirlwind had turned the place all higgledy-piggledy, with bookshelves knocked to the floor, a desk that leaned at a forty-five degree angle against the wall, and the contents of every file drawer and desk drawer scattered everywhere. While there was no sign of Sherry, her purse was among the disturbed contents within those four walls. Chipman saw it at the back of the room, its strap torn off and its leather outerskin crushed like a deflated football.

As he stepped cautiously through the debris, Chipman saw something glinting on the floor, something that blinked in sequence with the ceiling light and which animated the scene around him. Bending down, he picked up the object, which to all appearances was a hand mirror that had been dumped, along with everything else, from Sherry's purse. Light and shadow skittered across the reflecting surface of the mirror. This was all that Chipman could see at first. But as he inspected the object more closely he noticed that there was also a face in that mirror . . . and the face was not his own. Nor was it Sherry's face, exactly. But it was the face of something, some Sherry-like thing, some creature from which almost every vestige of Sherry had been distilled and only the Thing part remained. And it seemed to be screaming with what seemed to be a mouth full of craggy teeth that, seemingly, were trying to eat their way out of the mirror.

Chipman dropped the mirror to the floor immediately, instinctively. Then he started crushing it underfoot, stomping on it with the heel of his shoe until the mirror was only a collection of sharp, glittering fragments which he frantically kicked into every corner of the room, thereby dispersing the image of something that had quickened his breathing and made his eyes stare as if they could still see the face in the mirror.

Standing amid the tremulous shadows of that office – its furnishings all atilt, little slivers of a funhouse mirror still shining among the debris about him – Chipman appeared lost within the narrow corridors of dark reverie. But he was brought back to himself when, from somewhere in the chaos of Sherry Mercer's old office, the telephone began to ring. Chipman scrambled toward the source of that mad warbling sound, which was not at all like the friendly twitter he was used to hearing from the modern phones in the company's offices. He finally tracked the noise to its hiding place beneath a mound of file folders that littered the floor.

'Yeah,' said Chipman, abandoning the formal salutations of the workplace.

'Chipman?' asked the voice on the phone.

'Yes, this is he,' he said, laughing a little.

'Where's Sherry?'

'She's . . . I don't know, Richard. She's not in her office. Something's wrong here. The place looks like it's been ransacked and . . . well, her purse is here but . . . maybe you should see it for yourself.'

'All right, settle down.'

'I am settled down,' said Chipman.

'You don't sound like it.'

'Well, it's just that . . . there was something.'

'Listen to me, Chipman. I'm going to ask you a question, and you're going to answer with a simple yes or no. Besides the condition of Sherry's office and the fact that her purse is still there –'

'It's practically ripped apart. Someone must have –'

'Let me finish. Besides what you've told me, the ransacking and so forth, have you seen, or perhaps heard, anything else, anything . . . that might seem out of the ordinary?'

'Yes,' answered Chipman as instructed. 'I saw something.'

'That's good, you're doing fine. One more question – yes or no answer. What you saw, was it something that made you feel as if –'

'Richard, I thought I was losing my mind,' Chipman interjected.

'All right, that's good.'

'It's good that I thought I was losing my mind?' Chipman said almost belligerently.

'No. It's good that you told me the truth. Now, I want you to go home. Leave the building right away. Tomorrow morning there's going to be a meeting, and I want you to be there. Just watch yourself until then. Can you do that?'

'I think I can do that,' said Chipman without a hint of conviction.

'All right, then,' said Richard. 'One more thing –'

Then the phone went dead. Chipman tried to bring it back to life to call Richard back, but it was gone. Tossing the defunct receiver to the floor, Chipman said to himself, 'I'm going to go home now. Richard said I should go home.' Then he turned and saw what was written on the door of the office. The words were scored into the wood in precise block lettering, carved quite deeply. And they hadn't been there before, those words –

WORK NOT DONE.

Chipman suddenly charged the door and opened it, as if any hesitation might result in a loss of nerve that might keep him trapped in that office – looking at those words – forever. But on the other side of the door there was only another door.

WORK NOT DONE.

And behind him there was only a dark wall illuminated by a flickering light.

Chipman now seemed to be listening for something, perhaps the comforting sound of the vacuum cleaners being pushed across the carpeted hallways and among the cubicles of the company offices. He called for help, but there was no one who could hear him. Because he wasn't in the company offices any more. He really wasn't anywhere. Nevertheless, he kept calling for help . . . and he kept opening door after door: WORK NOT DONE, WORK NOT DONE, WORK NOT DONE . . .

After a while even I could no longer follow him into that place of endless doors and darkness.

Part III

1

MEMO TO: You
FROM: Me
DATE: Thursday Evening
SUBJECT: The Darkness

As many of you have already realized, I did not give up my intentions of crafting a document that, in an earlier section, I described as my Ultimate Statement. This document, or statement, had merely mutated into a different format – from a ranting declaration into what might be categorized as a paranormal memoir: a work-in-progress of uncertain form, very much like its creator. Among the principal elements to emerge in this latter form was that sinister presence whose sign and symbol had appeared to me as (1) a river of blackness; (2) a constellation of dark stars which filled the darkness *behind* the darkness of the night sky; (3) 'dark spots' that, despite my enhanced perception of the world around me, still obscured certain crucial things from my view, most prominently any knowledge concerning the peculiar – 'non-living' – state in which I now existed; and (4) stains or smudges of darkness which spread across the sky at all hours and grew increasingly prominent each time I knocked the living daylights out of one of The Seven (plus Chipman).

At the time specified above, it was the last of these four phenomena that most preoccupied me, given that I had eliminated no fewer than three persons before sundown (which, of course, was still an hour behind on the clocks in my time zone and would remain so for one more October day). Even during the later hours of Thursday afternoon, following my annihilation of Sherry Mercer and the man I knew as Harry Smith-Jones, the world outside my apartment windows was stuck in a shade of deep twilight as far as I could see.

The dark stains hovered in the sky above the old buildings of the downtown area and extended into the distance across the river, creating a cityscape that was so evenly overcast that it took on the phony look of a stage-setting or a day-for-night scene in a low-budget movie. Furthermore, sometime after I sent Chipman to his doom, there was a definite moment when things took on a still darker tint, as if to mark the precise time when the Young Supervisor could no longer deny to himself the heart-stopping fact that he would never find his way to the end of that infinite series of doors.

Clearly a pattern was discernable in these darkenings that came upon the heels of each act of uncanny mayhem that I worked upon my former colleagues. I wondered if this was a sign of one of those stupid rules that encumbered us all, living or non-living, a law of limitation that read: 'This far and no farther,' or possibly, 'This many and no more.' Anyhow, after a rather busy day of putting down bad beasts, I decided to pause that evening to reflect upon this pattern I had observed. As I lay, in bodily form, on the sofa in the living room of my apartment – that wonderfully bleak penthouse above Lillian's downtown diner – I roughly estimated that at the rate that these darkenings were encroaching on my world, I would be able to eliminate my remaining coworkers, that is my erstwhile coworkers, just before I myself was plunged into a realm of permanent and total darkness, sinking back into that metaphorical river of blackness from which I had, by means unknown to me, somehow escaped before I had become entirely submerged into its greasy waters.

This realization (if it wasn't purely a matter of imagination, I thought) was a disheartening one. Because as satisfying as I found my work of exterminating these vermin in whatever bizarre manner I could conceive, my mind had already begun turning toward bigger things, more elaborate schemes on a far greater scale. After all, the planet that I inhabited, the reality in which I was captured, was brimming with all kinds of potential victims, all of whom, to some degree, were swine that I dearly wanted to lead into my house of slaughter.

This feeling of mine, this passion, was absolutely confirmed and bolstered during those moments when I had occupied the body of Lillian Hayes for the purpose of liquidating, in a literal sense, Harry the Robber and Rapist. Now here was a woman who, I believed, was as decent as anyone could be, as close to being a non-swine as any human being could get. And yet all the time that I inhabited her physical body, I could feel how intimately that body – in both its physical and metaphysical aspects – was connected to that now familiar darkness, that sinister presence . . . a presence that might well have been named The Great Black Swine – a grunting, bestial force that animated, that *used* our bodies to frolic in whatever mucky thing came its way, lasciviously agitating itself in that black river in which the human species only bobbed about like hunks of excrement. Indeed, after inhabiting the body of another – in this case the body of Lillian Hayes – it seemed to me that the idea of a human species, of anything like a 'person' (or persons known or unknown) was only a figure of speech, a convenient delusion.

Then, sometime between dumping Harry in the soup and sending Chipman into a maddening oblivion, it occurred to me: *All of them must be done away with . . . everyone must go!*

And as I lay on the sofa in the living room of my apartment I could only lament that I would not be able to continue my work beyond The Seven (Chipman notwithstanding). A limit had been placed on my labors before the blackness would close in on me entirely. I was still being manipulated, I was still being crowded and conspired against by something beyond my control and frustrating to my Will. But then something happened, right in the living room of my apartment, that served to reconcile me to this situation, or at least instill in my soul a sense of grim resignation.

It took the form of a cockroach scuttling across the carpet. I jumped up from the sofa and, with a rapidity and precision that came along with my peculiar state of existence, I trapped the creature beneath my heavy black boot without killing it. Even through the thick sole of that boot I could feel the bug scuttling in place. At this point I was merely in physical connection with it. Next, I established a deeper communion with this vermin, letting a little bit of myself flow into its body, linking me to its life in the same manner that I had joined myself to Lillian Hayes. Although my immersion into the roach was not as complete as it had been with Lillian, I nonetheless felt the exact same sensation: there was nothing especially 'roachy' inside the roach any more than there was anything of a distinct 'person' inside of Lillian – once the dark interior of each had been penetrated, there was only that buzz of swinish agitation and turbulent blackness. The Great Black Swine was thrashing about inside the cockroach just as it had within Lillian Hayes, the only difference being that any sense of delusion about being some kind of thing-in-the-world was missing from the insect, or perhaps it was only so faint that I could not detect it.

Was it simply a matter of degree? Between the cockroach and the proprietor of the Metro Diner there spread quite a spectrum of organic life. Was there a corresponding spectrum of delusion about being things-in-the-world? For instance, I've noticed – and who hasn't? – that cats seem to regard themselves in a way very similar to that of humans ... and vice versa. 'Cats are people,' I heard the voice of an old woman speak from somewhere in my memory. And, from a feline perspective, people might very well seem to be cats. And inside of all of them – the thrashing agitation of the Devouring Swine, the Conspiratorial Swine, and, yes, the Murdering Swine. This was the only Thing-in-the-World. The rest of it was only costumes and masks, the inventory of an ancient and still flourishing theatrical supply company.

And they would all have to go – people, cats, roaches, plants, *all of it had to go*.

But I knew that I – whatever 'I' was – would not be the one to do it. The work was too immense, the scale of slaughter impossible to attain. The assurance that every speck of living matter had been swept from this world – and what about all the other worlds? – would have to remain in the realm of Never-To-Be ... the beatific dream of an obsessive-compulsive life form.

However, it was all over for the roach. When I pressed my boot down to the floor I could feel everything go still and silent within that little body where before there had been only a vicious thrashing in blackness. I even felt a little part of myself – the part of me I had allowed to leak into the bug – grow still and silent. It felt good. Very good, however fleeting the feeling had been. I can truly say that it was the only moment of real well-being I had ever experienced in my life, if my present state of existence could in fact be considered part of that fabrication I called my life.

And at that moment I was sure that I was still living in some way – that even if I was not entirely alive, neither was I wholly dead. Somehow I was caught in between these two worlds – caught in a place where I had made a rare connection with that Great Black Swine, that thrashing and vicious blackness which flowed like a river through every living thing, and possibly in the spaces around everything that lived, allowing me to be wherever the blackness flowed, to become one with this agitated force that was everywhere and inside everything, that moved and manipulated all the created life of this world and gave me the power to move and manipulate things according to my will, which was nevertheless only the lower-case will of an isolated being – a cockroach elevated to human form, a small swirling of that flowing blackness that was as great and enduring as the world itself, that was the secret face of the living world, the shadow within all life, the thing that would live on and on as each one of us died our deaths alone. Because whatever life we had was only *its* life, and when our bodies, our cockroach bodies, became too damaged to accommodate it . . . this blackness flowed away, leaving behind it a dead vine, a bug's crushed carapace, or a human corpse – things that had no life of their own, nothing real at all about them.

Yet if my life was all delusion, it was an inescapable delusion that I – and, alas, even you – could not fail to follow wherever it might lead. And I still had four more beings to blow away from this creepy existence. Until that was accomplished my work was not yet done, and my life (or non-life, as it were) seemed undeniably worth living. Somehow I had been given the power to finish the work I had begun when I entered that downtown gun shop to purchase a load of firearms and a Buck Skinner Hunting Knife.

I – and you – now understood: We were brought into this world out of nothing.

I – and you – now understood: We were kept alive in some form, any form, as long as we were viciously thrashing about, acting out our most intensely vital impulses, never allowed to become still and silent until every drop had been drained of the blackness flowing inside us.

I – and you – now understood: We would be pulled back into the flowing blackness only when we had done all the damage we were allowed to do, only when our work was done. The work of you against me . . . and me against you.

2

On Friday morning the homicide detectives were sitting in their unmarked car just down the street from the gun shop where once upon a time I had planned to pick up a few things. The store was supposed to open at ten o'clock, but they arrived a half-hour early. There they were, sipping coffees and lackadaisically eyeing whatever came into their field of vision. I was sitting – unseeable – in the back seat, thinking to myself, 'Do you really think that I'm going to make an appearance to pick up my order? You guys are either very thorough or very stupid.'

Then Detective White said something that put me in my place. 'You know we're wasting our time here, don't you?'

'Yup,' said Detective Black. 'No way he's going to show up.'

'You know why the lieutenant ordered this stakeout, don't you?'

'Yup. It's not like this is the first time.'

'But it still stinks.'

'Take it easy. Here, have a bagel,' said Detective Black as he reached into a paper bag.

Detective White took the bagel and tore into it like an angry dog. 'This isn't the place we should be. We should be questioning those execs at the company, with or without their lawyers.'

'That's not what the lieutenant wants.'

'That not what he wants because he got the word.'

'The word from the man who got the word from the man,' said Detective Black.

'You know how many people have stopped showing up for work at that place?'

'I know.'

'I'd like to have a talk with the ones that are still left,' said Detective White as his full set of remarkably square teeth tore off another hunk of bagel, and he continued to talk with his mouth full. 'They're the ones who know what's going on. I don't like it when people tell me that I shouldn't try to find out what's really going on.'

'You know the score,' said Detective Black. 'That's a big company. What's going on there is probably not good for their business.'

'They should let us do our job.'

'I agree.'

'People should know what really goes on in this city,' said Detective White.

'I'd like to know myself sometimes. But what can you do?'

'Nothing.'

'Want another bagel?' said Detective Black as he helped himself to one of the poppy-seed variety.

Detective White waved off seconds on the bagels and continued gazing lackadaisically through the windshield of the unmarked car.

If I hadn't already known what I knew about certain things, I might have thought to myself, 'You guys are . . .'

'All right, then,' said Richard to his gathered underlings in the usual meeting place. He had already tried to contact Chipman, both at home and at work, but he didn't seem surprised at the young man's absence. But what could he say to the others about Chipman, not to mention the empty chairs once occupied by Sherry and Harry? Come on, Richard, tell them what you know about Domino. Tell *me* what you know. Like Detective White, I wanted to know what was going on.

Mary and Kerrie were sitting to the left and right of Richard, while Barry had positioned himself at the far end of the table.

'Why don't you move in a little closer, Barry boy?' said Richard.

Covering her mouth, Mary whispered, 'He smells really bad, Richard. I think he's sick.'

'I'm, uh, fine where I am,' said Barry. And that ended the issue.

'So where do we go from here, Rich?' said a cocky Kerrie.

Richard eyed Kerrie as if she were a talking whippet, which in fact she resembled, and then spoke softly to her. 'You should probably be taking this situation more seriously, Kerrie.'

'I have no fear whatever of Frank Dominio. I just *wish* he'd try something with me. I'm ready,' she said, patting a slight bulge in the pocket of the sport coat she wore every day with a T-shirt, jeans, and athletic shoes.

'I'm afraid I can't say the same,' said Mary. 'Is there any point in bringing up the others who couldn't be with us today?'

'None at all, Mary,' said Richard with a business-like finality. 'What about you, Barry? Any apprehensions at your end of the table?'

Barry just stared without any focus like a lobotomy case. Then he sniffed, actually snorted, very loudly and scratched his armpit. He was clearly having a hard time following the proceedings. One – and that one would be me – might say that Barry was no longer his old brilliant self.

'Then what's the point of this meeting?' said Mary, her mask of make-up shining with perspiration. 'Everything, all our plans . . . what I mean to say is, it's over . . . isn't it?'

'It's not over until it's over,' spoke Richard. 'The important thing is to maintain appearances. None of us has anything to hide.'

'Oh, come on,' said Kerrie. 'Frank's out there doing us one by one. But we did *him* first.'

'We certainly didn't do any violence to him,' said Richard. 'We just wanted something that he had.'

'And once we got that – what? You're The Doctor, Richard. We know what that means.'

Richard sighed with infinite boredom. 'Is anyone here going to back Kerrie up in her accusations?'

Mary bit her lower lip, smearing her upper teeth with a layer of lipstick. Barry continued to scratch and sniff-snort. I still wanted Richard to tell them what he knew about Domino, but it was now obvious that this was not going to happen. The whole point of that meeting was damage control for Richard. And he knew, as I did, that the damage wasn't over.

3

My taste for the Grotesque was neither an inborn nor a longstanding trait of my character. Rather, it was conceived and developed over the period of time encompassed by this document, my Ultimate Statement. By Friday – the last Friday of October – this taste, which was already as ripe as the fruits of an autumn harvest, had finally gone thoroughly rotten. It was now an unslakeable hunger for unheard-of horrors, for all the derangements bred by the most morbid fevers, and for the stuff of nightmares so twisted, so aberrant, that they were beyond the comprehension or recall of the waking mind. Please let me show you – all of you – what I did that day. It began with –

Barry

Actually I had intended Barry, rather than Perry, as my first project, given that this waddling wretch had been Richard's primary tool in my decline and fall at the company. However, good sense overcame vengeful rage, and I decided to begin practicing on the piano player – whose annihilation may now be seen to have been a simple finger exercise compared to my later work – while saving the more choice subjects for later, when I had reached the height of my monstrous powers. Nevertheless, Barry remained a side-project for me from the beginning. His slow wit and strong odor at the meeting on Friday were merely superficial signs that this swine was ready for the market.

Barry left the office well before lunch. He no longer felt comfortable in such structured – correction, *restructured* – surroundings. All he wanted was to get back to his brick house (no house of straw or clay for this piggy), where things were just the way he now liked them.

As he drove his car through a winding route of city streets – he was no longer mentally competent to handle the high speeds and quick thinking required to maneuver on the expressway – the only thoughts in his head were images of home. (This place, to describe it with a minimum of foul details, was a sty ... literally.) These images which now filled Barry's beasty brain, since his ability to think in words and concepts had almost entirely atrophied, consisted wholly of wallowing in filth, which included the remains of the filth that he heaped *into* his body as well as the filth that emanated out of that same body and was spread over every inch of his floor and furnishings. Barry's brick bungalow was truly hog heaven. And he could hardly wait to strip off his human clothes and roll his flabby, naked flesh around in the slop, snorting and squealing all the while.

But Barry's mind was not yet so intellectually impaired that he couldn't make a few stops at the drive-though windows of several fast-food joints on his way home, filling both the front and back seats of his car with bags and bags of burgers, tacos, and crusty hunks of fried chicken. It was at his last stop (a rib shack!) that Barry caught the scent of something else that tantalized his tastes, although it was not something he could eat.

It so happened that Barry's drive home led him directly past the state fairgrounds, which were now in the full swing of a fall exhibition that included a midway of concession stands bursting with corn dogs and cotton candy, an amphitheater that filled the air with country music, and the usual showing of agricultural products from both field and barnyard. This was Barry's lucky day ... and mine. Without thinking twice, or even once, Barry pulled his car into the fairground's parking lot, and, after gobbling a bag or so of sustenance, he wandered into the festive world of the fair. He was following that overpowering scent and, in his blind search, he disappeared into the crowd ... disappeared forever.

The only hint of what might have become of Barry Edwins was an item that appeared the next day in the city's major newspaper and was reprinted in several other publications in outstate regions. The facts were these:

First: Someone reported to the police who were keeping order at the state fair that she had seen a naked man trying to couple with a prize pig featured at a livestock exhibition.

Second: When the police arrived at the exhibition, that nasty, naked man was nowhere to be found. What they did find, however, was a rape in progress ... but it was the act of a pinkish hog upon a blue-ribbon sow.

Third: No one could be found who would claim the offending hog as theirs. One old livestock breeder did note that the genitalia of the hog, while quite small, were still intact. That is, this was an animal that had not been properly fixed for its breed and ultimate purpose.

Last: Granted permission by the police to do what needed to be done (in exchange for taking ownership of this rather fine specimen of its type), the old livestock breeder castrated the animal on the spot in order to bring it under control and promised that, by and by, this handsome hog would find a home at a good slaughterhouse.

To commemorate this turn of events I directed a – blech! – email message to Richard's computer under the subject line of, what else, WORK NOT DONE. But I was denied the satisfaction of seeing Richard read this message. In fact, I seemed to have lost the ability to locate him altogether. This was something that threw a scare into me. Because there was only one place that he could have hidden himself from my view. Somehow Richard had gone into a dark spot, but I couldn't be sure why or how this had happened. Hadn't I always been given free rein to do my work? Never mind, I told myself, there was other work to be done. And there she was –

Mary

After the mess that the cleaning staff found in Sherry Mercer's office, Mary tried to spend as little time as possible in her own ... or anywhere else in the company's office space if she could help it. Her heels were now clicking upon the sidewalks of downtown toward her favorite lunch spot, which would be filled with a crowd of people among whom she would feel relatively safe.

However, as – not *luck* but I – would have it, Mary walked right by her destination. And she kept on walking toward the outskirts of the business section of the city, wandering through rundown neighborhoods and past many of my once favorite ruined buildings (including an old place that still had a sign in the window that read: 'Rooms for Men'). But my feeling for these places was a thing of the past for me. The soothingness of *sabi*, with its mind-clearing desolation and soul-calming decrepitude, had now been replaced by my taste for the Grotesque. Nothing but the Grotesque would gratify my howling mind and poisoned soul. Only the Grotesque.

So I took Mary out of the range of vast empty fields and beautifully gutted buildings, dropping her off at a place known as The Mechanic Street Museum. This nominal 'museum' was spread out along a block of abandoned houses not far from a railroad overpass and across the road from a dumping ground for old sofas and chairs, old tires, old medicine cabinets, and any other expired object you cared to name. The exhibits of the museum consisted entirely of old dolls and mannikins, or the various parts of same. These human simulations inhabited both the interior spaces of each abandoned house as well as populating their front yards. Behind any given window, often shattered, of the houses along this section of Mechanic Street, one might see an entire mannikin – sometimes clothed or partially clothed and sometimes not – or at least part of a mannikin, such as a slim forearm and hand held in place by some putty on the inside window sill. Additionally, these windows might display a doll hanging by its neck as if from a gibbet, or simply the head of a doll dangling at the end of a wire.

This community of dolls and mannikins also lounged upon the wooden porches, or the steps leading up to these porches, and sometimes peered out from the exposed crawlspaces beneath a number of the abandoned houses. Most interesting were the dolls and mannikins that had been set up in old chairs or sofas taken from the dumping ground across the street. The dolls leaned crookedly in chairs that were invariably too large for them, while the mannikins lay in twisted postures upon sofas without cushions. No one had ever claimed credit for creating this museum, which had attained modest renown in both local publications and nationally distributed art journals. Nor had anyone ever been caught, though many had tried, in the act of augmenting its exhibitions, filling the Mechanic Street houses and their yards with still more dolls and mannikins and replacing the ones that had become too damaged, either by vandals or the elements, to remain on display.

As I earlier explained, Mary Dreller had been led astray into the region of The Mechanic Street Museum while on her way to an out-of-office lunch. No one at the company noticed that she had not logged off her computer, and it was assumed that she, not unlike Barry Edwins, had left work early that Friday. It wasn't until later the same night that her husband reported her to the police as a missing person. The police, of course, would never find Mary but I will tell you – whoever you are or think you are – just who did find her and where she was found.

* * *

It was a few hours after sunset (EDT) that a couple of derelicts, both of them drunken and deranged, were passing through The Mechanic Street Museum. They had covered this ground before and were not daunted by its peculiar aspects. Quite the opposite, in fact. Pausing in front of a house where a doll's head stared from a high attic window, the derelicts parked themselves on either side of a sofa near the sidewalk. Between them was a fully clothed mannikin sitting up with fair posture, although her head was twisted over the back of the sofa. Out of all the mannikins these derelicts had ever seen loitering in the vicinity, this one came closest to something that could be mistaken for a human being.

'Must be a new one,' said the first derelict.

'Yeah,' said the other. 'But – uuurrp – lookit her face.'

As drunken and deranged as the derelicts were, even they could not overlook the flaw in this window dummy. Specifically, its face did not display the requisite expression of bland beatitude but, on the contrary, was severely contorted – the face of something that was frozen in a moment of panic.

'I bet we could get something for these clothes,' said the first derelict, running his dirty hands from top to bottom over the mannikin's body. 'It's got stockings even.'

'Let's take off her clothes,' said the other.

As the derelicts proceeded to undress the mannikin, they were further amazed that it was outfitted with undercloth-ing. The first derelict started talking to the dummy, calling her Daisy, and then the other derelict joined in the fantasy. One thing led to another . . . and by the time Daisy was fully rid of her clothes, the derelicts had laid this fake lady of the evening across the sofa and began taking turns on top of her. That night there was a full moon over Mechanic Street and these derelicts were evidently in the mood for a little messing around, even if their object of desire was merely a mannikin, although one that might be easily mistaken, as she had been for years, for a human being.

Then one of the derelicts suddenly jumped off the dummy, stumbling backward with his pants around his ankles. 'Her eyes,' he said. 'They . . . they were looking back at me.'

The other derelict, zipping himself up, stepped closer to the thing spread out on the cushionless sofa. 'Oh, my god,' he groaned.

Then both of the derelicts, having pushed the mannikin onto the sidewalk, began stomping on her face and assaulting her body with a piece of metal pipe that was lying on the ground nearby. What they found inside the mannikin turned out to be even more distressing to them than her contorted face or her eyes that looked back into theirs. For beneath its plaster exterior was an anatomically correct set of bodily organs, even if they too seemed to be made of artificial materials. If the derelicts had had the presence of mind, or any useful minds at all, they might have rationalized this horrific figure as a construct intended for use in the medical school at the university, which was only a few miles away. Instead they kept pummeling away at the unnatural thing, especially its face, until nothing remained but a heap of shattered plaster. They even left its clothes behind as they broke into a breathless, stumbling flight from The Mechanic Street Museum.

While the episode with Mary was quite a success, if somewhat lacking in imagination (I had already used the mannikin theme in dispatching Perry Stokowski), the satisfaction I derived from its grotesquerie was undermined by my continuing failure to locate Richard. I had always intended him to be the last of The Seven upon whom I would visit my wrath. Now I was beginning to worry that something was wrong. Visions of a doctor with great white gloves were beginning to disturb my – let's admit it – hopelessly disturbed mind. I left a message of WORK NOT DONE on the voice mail of both his home phone and his cell phone. But Richard was not picking up my communications, I could tell. Forget it, I told myself. You – and you was me – should be turning your attention to the penultimate person on the list –

Kerrie

I found her sometime after midnight. She was parking her car in front of a club that – big surprise – catered to patrons of sadomasochistic impulses.

The club, which displayed no sign to betray its name or nature, was located in the warehouse district not far from the river and was set up in a battered old building that I once might have looked upon as a ruin suitable for my meditations and my camera. But this building was alight with a hazy red glow, a private place halfway along a pitted road without streetlamps and under a sky that, for me in any case, was filled only with those dark constellations which put a black-out on all the stars above. And after my self-designed run-in with Kerrie, the sky would become even darker.

Despite the sadomasochistic rationale for the club's existence, its decor had nothing of the oubliette about it, nothing at all to distinguish it as a palace of pain and humiliation. Some paper pumpkins and skulls had been strung over a small bar in anticipation of the upcoming All Hallows, although in every other respect it resembled an old-fashioned neighborhood saloon. Like the company where I was once employed, the owner of this operation was obviously dedicated to the standard business principle of offering his clientele the least (a few tables and chairs, some wobbly stools along the bar) for the most (a sky-high cover charge and outrageously priced drinks from the bottom of their respective barrels). Even this purported haven for the deviant, the outsider, functioned along the mainstream goal of commerce, always aiming for the fiscal ideal of everything for them, the sellers and sellers-out of the world, and zero for . . . well, everyone was 'them' to me now, at least in the sense that neither corporate nor even *corporeal* dealings were any longer my business.

Or so I told myself, even though the whole picture was not mine to see . . . and somewhere in the darkness of that October night, Richard was still hiding from me in some dark spot where I could not find him, as I had so easily tracked down Kerrie to this hole-in-the-wall hangout. And I needed to find him – to finish up my work – before everything became for me one great world of darkness. Yet I continued to believe that my calculations were correct – the damage that was given to me to do was compounded at a fixed rate. And there remained enough principal in my account of worldly existence for me to complete the task I had started – none of The Seven (or myself) would ever see another sunrise; none of us would reclaim that hour which had been stolen by the daylight savings of the previous spring and was not scheduled to be returned for approximately another twenty-four hours or so. But what was an hour . . . a day . . . a year or ten? There's always plenty of time for the worst. Everyone is old enough to face their fate.

And so was Kerrie Keene.

She had just walked in the door, carrying in one hand a leather bag that was not a purse. Wearing her usual outfit, she swaggered toward the far end of the bar and leaned over to ask the barman, 'Is The Can here yet?'

'He's waiting for you downstairs,' said the barman as he tossed Kerrie a key dangling at the end of a red plastic disc.

Kerrie immediately strode toward a curtained doorway that led downstairs, which was a complex of rooms set up like a subterranean motel . . . and a very cheap motel at that. After moving down several hallways, turning left here and right there without the least hesitation, she stopped at a certain door and let herself in.

On the other side was a small bare room that appeared in the same light of garish red that illuminated the bar upstairs and the corridors below. In the shadows of one corner of the room a short, flabby man was on his knees with lowered head, as if he were praying. He didn't even look up when Kerrie stormed into the room and slammed the door behind her. And he didn't look up when Kerrie threw her leather bag on the floor and stripped off her sport coat, revealing two skinny arms springing forth from a sleeveless T-shirt.

'Hello, Can,' she said to the man in the corner, who still did not raise his eyes to her. 'I've brought something special for you tonight.'

'Can,' I already knew from previous research (I had always been thorough in my work), was a pseudonym that to Kerrie, and to most of those around the SM scene, was short for Human Garbage Can. But before Kerrie could begin making use of this living receptacle, packing it full of that special sort of offal she had brought with her this night, she realized something was wrong: The Can seemed to have gone stiff as a statue. None of the usual words of worship and submission that Kerrie was accustomed to hearing at this point in the ritual were uttered by the short, flabby, and naked man. She walked across the floor and laid several slaps, both backhand and forehand, on The Can's pudgy face. But there was no response from the figure still postured as though in silent prayer.

Then the door opened, and I walked into the room in all my black attire, including a zippered leather mask over my face.

'You've got the wrong room, Masked Man. Take a walk.'

The Masked Man stood heroically mute and perfectly rigid, staring at Kerrie through a pair of eye-holes with thick, almost surgical, stitching around them. Then he reached into his coat pocket and took out something small and circular, tossing it into Kerrie's hands. The second she realized it was a fresh roll of stamps, she moved toward her sport coat that had made a clunk when she first threw it on the floor. The Masked Man was quicker than Kerrie and pushed her against the wall, being careful not to push too hard, before she could retrieve her weapon. Then The

Masked Man moved with all speed and pulled the firearm from Kerrie's jacket.

It was a Glock.

And it felt so fine in my fingers as I clicked off the safety and aimed the barrel at Kerrie's head. She had pressed her body flush against the cinder-block wall, standing as if before a firing squad. This was how I had originally imagined my work would be done. If it hadn't been for . . . paper? I was sick of having my mind harassed by paper moons and paper plates, paper products of all kinds both figurative and literal. Why couldn't I break through those dark spots and remember? Everything could have been so much easier, so much quicker, and far less grotesque for everyone concerned if things had only gone according to plan. Even now I was tempted to install the full magazine of the gun into Kerrie's body and leave it at that. But I already had other plans in place. I had been thorough, as always, in my research.

'Do you know why he's called The Can?' I asked Kerrie.

'Go to hell. Why don't you just shoot?'

'I asked you if you knew, *really* knew, why he's called The Can?'

'He pretends he's a garbage can. He eats . . . he eats whatever you put in his mouth. He swallows it and begs for more.'

'Do me a favor and move a little closer to Mr Can,' I said, directing her toward the paralyzed figure in the corner. 'Closer still, Kerrie. Right up against his body, as if you were riding him piggy-back. There, that's close enough.'

'Close enough for what?' she asked, a satisfying quiver of fear in her voice.

Then I set my plans in motion . . . and her body began to sink down into his. She struggled. She even screamed. But this was not a place where screams were taken seriously at first. Besides, the door was heavy, and it was locked. I continued my conversation with Kerrie as a monologue, since she was sinking fast into the flabby man's flesh and had begun choking on her own horror.

'You're right about Mr Can. He does eat whatever you, or someone like you, puts in his mouth. But he also eats other things. He's not just a garbage can, Kerrie. What you never knew about Mr Can is that not only does he have a secret life that he lives out in places like this. He also has a *secret* secret life that he would never have told you about. By night he's the human garbage can you know but probably do not love. In an even darker night of his soul, Mr Can is . . . he's, well there's just no subtle way I can say this. He's a cannibal. And soon you're going to be made one with him – your brain buried inside of his brain, your nervous system integrated into his, and your desires bound to his desires. Unfortunately you will be denied all muscular control. You'll exist something like a parasitic organism inside him. A tapeworm if you like. But he won't be bothered by you. He'll continue to eat as you've always known him to eat. And you will know that you are eating the same things. He will also eat as you never knew him to eat. There are others like him, and he is in league with them. Mostly they consume homeless persons who have fallen unnoticed by the wayside. Sometimes they give them a little help in their going. On rare occasions they eat living food. Are you aware of the word that cannibals who once occupied islands in the South Pacific used for "human being?" It translates as "the food that talks". Mr Can and others of his kind live to eat. I know that was never your style, Kerrie, but from now on it will be . . . as long as Mr Can lives. And you know what: he's even made special preparations with his fellow cannibals for the day when he will be too dead to chew his food. It seems to be their desire, don't ask me why, that after their demise they be buried naked in secret ground. After their life of eating is over, their final wish is to become food for other forms of life. It's rather spiritual, don't you think? The great circle of being and all that. Of course, just because Mr Can is dead doesn't necessarily mean that you'll join him. You're so much younger, so much healthier – even given your anorexic mania – than he is. I'm guessing that the little parasite inside him will outlive his body by a certain term, although I can't say how long that will be. Can you still hear me, Kerrie? You're sliding down into him so fast. It's almost as if you can't wait to get inside. Prick up your ears if you'd like to hear more.'

But she was gone. And so was I.

'Wake up, Mr Can,' I said to the man in the corner just before I left the room.

4

After leaving Kerrie and Mr Can behind in that shed-like room, I sent out my last message to Richard (WORK NOT DONE, in case you forgot), using every possible means of communication, including the barking dog in the backyard next to Richard's house, some writing in chalky deodorant on his bathroom mirror, and even telepathy, which I knew from the beginning of this whole heinous saga was not a strength of mine. But once again I failed to raise him by wireless means. And I still could not locate his position on my radar.

The streets outside were now so death-darkened that I could no longer make my way on foot. Even when I switched to travelling by means of spectral byways, at which I had become so adept, I found that I was no longer master of these roads. All the routes that were familiar to me seemed to have changed, mostly into a series of dead-ends. I felt as if I were trying to negotiate a maze that was not taking me where I wanted to go but where it wanted me to go. And when I finally reached what I thought was the way to freedom, I discovered that I was still not outside the maze but at its very center. And that center was the old meeting room which was outside company space, even if it was deep inside the world of Richard the Minotaur.

I reassumed worldly appearances and opened the door to the room. While always dim, the place had never looked dimmer to my eyes than it did at that moment. Nevertheless, I ventured across the floor of the room in corporate form. I walked to the table in corporate form. And in corporate form I took a seat at that table where, at the opposite end, sat Richard.

'I'm glad you made it here,' he said.

'I don't think I had much choice.'

'But this is where you want to be. Nothing else really matters any more.'

'I'm glad you're resigned to the facts.'

'You mean because you're here to do some terrible deed?'

'My very worst,' I said, although not as convincingly as I would have liked.

'Your worst, I'm sure. All because I made you feel bad. That really proves it – you haven't learned anything. And after what you've been through.'

'Illusions don't die that easily. Whatever I've learned doesn't really matter. I'm still Domino as long as you exist.'

'You mean as long as *you* exist.'

'That's right. You said that you knew I wasn't a dead man.'

'Oh, that was just some simple detective work.'

'Then why wasn't it done by the real detectives?'

'Because they didn't know what I knew. They had you down from the start as a suspect in Perry's ... Before I forget – why the mannikin hands? That was fairly crude.'

'I thought it appropriate. What's the difference? All right, I didn't know how far I could take things at the time. Now tell me what it was the detectives didn't know.'

'It was an assumption they made. Considering what happened to Perry, they naturally thought that you were up and around in the usual manner of mad-dog murderers. How could they know that this was rather far from the case? When they ran the check on your credit card purchases the day you were . . . the day you resigned, they quite reasonably focused on your visit to the gun shop. They didn't consider it important that you later picked up a few things at that office supply store, although they did ask me if *I* thought this was significant. But I just shrugged like an innocent.'

I must have given Richard the blankest look in the world when he started talking about the office supply store. I remembered buying the guns; I remembered buying the clothes. I remembered suddenly being back in my apartment that night – how confused I was, and how I was in such a terrible funk because I didn't know whether I was alive or dead. I didn't think I had the strength to pick up a piece of paper . . . and the idea of paper left a chilling echo in my mind.

'Do you see now? You weren't able to remember buying those reams of paper,' Richard continued. 'It's strange how some things are just blocked from your brain.'

'What would you know about that?'

'Not as much as you, I'm sure. But I do have your interest now, don't I? So you're going to listen to me crow about how I deduced what became of little Domino.'

'I don't have to listen to anything,' I said, pulling my Buck Skinner Hunting Knife from my pocket and laying it on the table.

'Wow. That *is* a real hand-chopper. There are some people I'd like to use that on myself. Do you think you're the only one who has scores to settle? It's not a question of whether the punishment fits the crime, is it? Not to swines like us. It's just a matter of getting that pain out of your system . . . and into someone else's. It's a dark world. Nothing but darkness. And whose business is it but our own what goes on in the dark?'

I wanted to be calm and menacing. I wanted to be a creature of murder-lust, a monster of all madnesses. I wanted to do things to Richard that would make the sun grow cold with horror. But I couldn't help following his script. 'Naturally I have my confusions about what I am, what I became. But I didn't expect to find myself wondering what on earth *you* are.'

'Me?' said Richard. 'I'm a person just like you. Well, not exactly like you. You're a miracle man. You didn't know that. A medical marvel. As I was saying, once your presence at the office supply store was established, it only remained to check out in the local papers if anything else of interest had happened around those corners that night.'

As Richard spoke these words a deafening sound came into my head. The sound of crashing and crunching, of metal and bone and screams and screams and screams. Then the sound of a roaring black river.

'It was a bus, Frank. The last of the line for the night. The driver was fully exonerated, if you care to know. You ran like a big black bird right in front of him, as several eye-witnesses told the officers at the scene. You were literally mashed to a pulp, completely unrecognizable as a human being, let alone anyone in particular . . . especially since you weren't carrying any identification on your person. That wasn't very smart.'

'Then I *am* a dead man,' I said aloud to myself.

'Everyone who saw that gruesome accident thought you were. Some of them said they didn't know which was worse – seeing your body all smeared and twisted in ways no one should have to see . . . or finding out that you were still alive. Comatose, but alive. I visited you a few times. Of course there wasn't – I'm sorry, *isn't* – anything to see but a heap of bandages. And a rather small heap at that, blood pooling through the gauze. But the fascinating part was the brain waves you were putting out on the EEG. Before I got there, they didn't think there was any point in hooking you up to it. But I can play a pretty convincing medicine man when I want to. I told them I was a specialist and that I'd known cases like this before. You should have seen the look on their faces when that monitor started skipping and jumping all over the place. That was when I knew you were going to be a problem for me.'

'How could you know that?'

'That's a strange question coming from you, Domino. I might just as well ask how you knew how to do the things you did. I'm not requesting details. I heard Chipman's voice when he described Sherry Mercer's office. He saw something in there that I *never* want to know about. And that's not even considering what became of the young man himself. It was bad enough getting those "work not done" messages whenever another one of the group seemed to just disappear. But I knew what I was getting myself into when I hired you. You and the rest of them. But it was you, Frank. You were the blackest of the bunch. I could see it in you from the start. Believe me, I know all about it. We – all of us – are the darkness that dreams are made on. I'm not claiming that I'm special in any way. It doesn't take anything more than a pair of clear eyes to see what makes the world go 'round. I've known about it since I was a child. Was it my fault that I liked to stare into the shadows until they started to stare back into me? That I performed little operations on stray animals? I really did want to be a doctor at that time in my life. But when I put my hands inside those creatures I never expected to feel what was really in there. It wasn't until I was older that I knew what I had felt inside them was also inside of me – that there wasn't anything else inside except that darkness. I thought about killing myself . . . but that wasn't the way for me. It had other plans for my life, and there wasn't much I could do except carry them out. It's my kind that calls the shots in this world, but we didn't ask for the job. Most of the time we think we're making our own agendas, following assignments that come from our own brains . . . or "from above", almost never from below, except perhaps in those strictly legendary instances wherein some poor boob thinks he's made himself a deal with the devil. What a load of crap that is. I'm not looking for your sympathy, Frank. Wouldn't that be deranged? I just wanted you to know that I have some idea of what you've been up to, not to mention up against, these past few days. It was strange what happened with you, but I don't think it was an accident. Most people have no idea what goes on in this world. But you know what it likes. It likes fear and agitation and conflict and all that stuff that makes such good copy for those folks who are selling that sort of thing – never mind all the sideliners whose happy lot is merely to peek in the window of the torture shop of life. I wanted you to know that I knew about that too. That's all I had to say. So what now?'

'I've gotten very good lately at coming up with fates worse than death. How about one of those?' I said. But my words sounded hollow even to me. I was still afraid, not of Richard himself, but of what was inside him, of what had been using him, and myself, as such obliging organisms for the most vicious and sinister acts.

'You can do whatever you want to me, sure,' he said. 'But unless I'm completely out of touch with things, you just barely made it here. And you're looking at me as if I'm standing in a black fog. Do you think you can do what you want to me and still make it to your next stop? That's where all of this is really heading for you, isn't it? Come on, you can't lie to me.'

He was right of course. I couldn't lie to him. But I didn't think I needed to lie.

'I believe you're right, Richard. What happened to me wasn't an accident. And it won't be over until my allotted body count is tallied up. There were seven of you.'

'Correct. And it was seven that you took. You didn't think about Chipman, did you? He never made much of an impression on anyone. But he was the joker I planted in the deck. If you waste the last bit of light you have left on me you'll never make it to where you want to go. It's a terrible choice you have to make. I'm sure you'd like to step into the blackness inside me and dance around in it with that big knife of yours. That's the real bad guy, and we both know it. That black stuff. But what can we do about it? We're just pictures painted on the darkness. Go and save yourself, Domino, if saving yourself still means anything to you. To tell you the truth, I'm fed up with the whole thing. You can do whatever you want.'

I suspected that Richard's words were only part of an act to save himself. I was sure of it when he asked me, 'By the way, whatever happened to that document of your idea, your special plan? Just out of curiosity. I don't really expect to see it.'

I was in a position that was frustrating beyond endurance. The worst of the swine was the one I had to let go. It seemed I had truly been beaten while he would continue to flourish.

'I'll tell you this, Richard. Keep watch on your computer screen. I'll send you something soon.'

Having said that, I put my knife back in my pocket and began my crawl along the lines of darkness that would lead me to only one place, one little room.

5

There he was, that bundle of bleeding bandages. The EEG was still active, portraying alarming surges of brain activity and glowing with an eerie incandescence. It was only by the colored lights of the medical appliances in that room that I could see anything at all. He looked like a mummy of someone whose every limb had been amputated to some extent. Tubes trailed out of a bandaged stump that had once been a whole arm as well as from the wrappings which suggested a shapeless head beneath. A catheter snaked its way from under a blanket, dribbling into a plastic bag hung on the side of the bed.

At the nurses' station down the quiet hallway there was a bulletin board which had pinned to it some newspaper clippings that pertained to this patient: the initial accident report (with a diagram), the investigation into the driving record of the guy at the wheel of that bus, the awful revelation that the victim still lived despite the incredible trauma sustained during the mishap, and a 'search goes on' piece that put out a call to anyone who might be able to provide information that could identify the man who lay in a coma at Memorial Hospital. The bent frames of a pair of wire-rimmed eyeglasses that might have belonged to the unknown man had been found some distance from his body, but the lenses had either popped out or were lost among the shattered debris of the accident.

And you were right, Richard. It was not an accident at all. As I looked down on that remnant of a human body I was finally able to remember what happened.

Rushing back to the office supply store to collect my forgotten packs of paper, I was very much preoccupied with the statement, my Ultimate Statement, that would eventually blacken those empty pages and eject them from the printer in my apartment. But the substance of this document still remained confused in my mind, its message frail and without force, its theme trite: 'They made me feel bad,' to paraphrase your own words, Richard, 'so I bought some guns and killed them all.' Such a statement, no matter how detailed and lengthy, simply would not do. I realized that even as I was running down the sidewalk to make it back to the office supply store before it closed. And I also knew that no words of greater weight or reason would occur to me once I had returned home. In a fraction of a second I became sick with the idea of sitting before my computer screen and tapping the same message over and over with only the slightest variations on the theme of 'they made me feel bad, so I bought some guns and killed them all'. There was nothing in such a statement except self-humiliation, self-ridicule, and self-indictment. Anyone reading it would have thought, 'What a worthless piece of human wreckage. And what a shame about those seven people.' There would have been no salvation for me in making such a statement, in committing such an act.

But then I saw my salvation speeding down the street in the form of a bus headed for the suburbs. I picked up my pace. I raced toward the only salvation that I knew was available to me. And I timed it perfectly.

By killing myself I felt that I would also be killing all of you, killing every bad body on this earth. To my mind, at that moment, every swinish one of us in this puppet show of a world would be done with when that bus made contact with me. Every suicide is a homicide – or many homicides – thwarted. My rage, my inner empire of murderous hate, had never been so intense as in those moments before I met that oncoming bus. Soon my statement would be made, not with words but with the violent action which is the only thing anyone really attended to, if only for a day or so. And the theme of my statement: 'To whom it may concern – I hereby refuse to be a swine living in a world of swine that was built by swine and belongs only to swine. This swine has been fed full of his swinish ambitions, his swinish schemes, and, over and above all, his swinish fears and obsessions. Therefore I forfeit my part of this estate to my heirs in the kingdom of the swine.'

That would seem to have been the end of it. I never suspected that I was going to be put to further use. I never suspected that there was a grander – if not exactly 'grand' – scheme of things. Not for a moment did I consider that I would continue to be manipulated and conspired against ... that I would become the instrument of greater manipulations and conspiracies, all the while being kept in the dark about what was really going on, about what should have been the real subject of my Ultimate Statement, as I now attempt to deliver it to you, not one of whom will ever benefit from it. People do not know, and cannot face, the things that go on in this world, the secret nightmares that are suffered by millions every day ... and the excruciating paradox, the nightmarish obscenity of being something that does not know what it is and yet believes that it does know, something that in fact is nothing but a tiny particle that forms the body of The Great Black Swine Which Wallows in a Great River of Blackness that to us looks like sunrises and skyscrapers, like all the knotted events of the past and the unraveling of these knots in the future, like birthdays and funerals, like satellites and cell phones and rockets launched into space, like nations and peoples, like the laws of nature and the laws of humanity, like families and friends, like everything, including these words that I write. Because this document, this supposedly Ultimate Statement, is only a record of incidents destined for the garbage can of the incredible. And rightly so. These incidents are essentially no different from any others in the world: they occurred in a particular sequence, they were witnessed and sometimes documented, but in the end they have no significance, no sense, no meaning, at least as I – and you and you and you – imagine these vacuous concepts.

All that remains to me, to my comatose body lying in a darkened hospital room, is to put an end to the thing beneath all those bandages. I'm sure that I'll be allowed to do so. My work is finally done. Yet having gone to all the trouble to concoct this statement, I cannot resist the ludicrous temptation to throw it out to the crowd. I told Richard I would send him something on his computer, although it won't be the documentation for a New Product idea, which I destroyed in both its digital and hard-copy forms. And whatever satisfaction it may bring Detectives White and Black, I will also forward a copy to them, so that they can match the fingerprints on the handle of this knife I hold over my own body to those that wait for them in my apartment . . . and so that they may know something of the atrocious wonders of this world. On Monday morning all the printers in the company will be spewing out these useless pages. Perhaps this occurrence will bring on the bad publicity which those merchants of stale information, those data pushers, so anxiously desire to avoid, since the company is now struggling for its life in the corporate arena. I am now struggling for my death. That's the only thing that matters.

I do not regret having annihilated seven persons any more than the fact that I'll never regain that lost hour which was taken from me six months ago. I make no excuses for my acts, and I beg no forgiveness or reprieve for the lives I've eliminated.

A curse on *them*.

These are the words of a swine who seeks only his own slaughter under the slicing, serrated blade of a Buck Skinner Hunting Knife.

A curse on *me*.

I was weak and afraid . . . and I ended up as a deadly weapon wielded by a dark hand that not even I – that no one – will ever see.

A curse on *it*.

I remember how wonderful it felt to die the little death of that cockroach in my apartment. I can only hope to know that feeling to its fullest when the moment comes and the river rushes in to drown me in its blackness. Perhaps a swine whose savage work is finally done may be allowed this much. I cannot wait to tear into the tender flesh of my last victim, and with a single slash kill two.

I cannot wait to be dead. I cannot wait.

I am not afraid any more.

I HAVE A SPECIAL PLAN FOR THIS WORLD

I remember working in an office where the atmosphere of tension had become so severe and pervasive that one could barely see more than a few feet in any direction. This resulted in considerable difficulties for those of us who were trying to perform the tasks which our jobs required. For instance, if for some reason we needed to leave our desks and negotiate our way to another part of the building, it was not possible to see beyond a certain distance, which was at most a few feet. Outside of this limited perimeter – this 'cocoon of clarity', as I thought of it – everything became obscured in a kind of quivering blur, an ambience of agitation within which the solid and dreary decor of the company offices appeared quite distorted.

People were constantly bumping into each other in the narrow aisleways and high-ceilinged hallways of the Blaine Company offices, so severe was this state of affairs in which the atmosphere of tension at that place had caused any object more than a few feet away to be lost in a jittering and filmy tableau. One might glimpse some indistinct shape nearby, perhaps something resembling a face, which at best would look like a rubber mask. Then suddenly you found yourself colliding with one of your fellow office workers. At that moment the image of the other person became grotesquely clarified in contrast to the otherwise blurry environment brought on by the severe tension, the incredible agitation that existed in the office and pervaded its every corner, even into the smallest storage room and the sub-basement of the old office building in which the Blaine Company was the only tenant.

After one of those collisions between coworkers, which occurred with great frequency during this time of tension, each of the persons involved would quickly mouth some words of pardon to the other. Of course I can only be sure about my own words – they were always polite expressions of self-pardoning, no matter how I actually felt at that precise moment of collision. As for the words that were spoken by the other person, I cannot attest, because these were invariably garbled or sometimes entirely lost in that same atmosphere of tension and agitation that obtained throughout the Blaine workplace. (Even in the closest quarters all exchanges of conversation carried only a few inches at most before they turned into a senseless babble or were lost altogether.) But whatever these words might have been was irrelevant, for very soon you had collected yourself and were rushing off once again into the blurred spaces before you in the Blaine offices, trying to put out of your mind that intensely clarified image you had witnessed, if only for a flashing moment – that microscopically detailed eyeball, that pair of super-defined lips (or just a single one of those lips), a nostril bristling with tiny hairs, a mountainous knuckle. Whatever you might have seen you wanted only to drive from your mind as soon as possible. Otherwise this image of some part of a human face or a human body would hook itself into your brain and become associated with the viciously tense and agitated state in which we all existed, thereby initiating a series of violent thoughts and fantasies concerning that eyeball or pair of lips, especially if you recognized the person to whom those parts were attached and could give a name to the object of your murderous rage.

To a certain extent the conditions I have described could be attributed to the management system under which the company was organized. It seemed evident that the various departmental supervisors, and even upper-level managers, operated according to a mandate that required them to create and maintain an environment of tension-filled conflict among the lower staff of the company. Whether this practice was dictated by some trend in managing technique or was endemic to the Blaine Company was a matter of speculation. But there was another, and more significant, reason for this climate of tense agitation under which we labored, a situation that, after all, is common to working environments everywhere. The reason to which I refer is this: the city in which the Blaine Company offices were located – in fact had very recently *re*-located – had once been known, quite justly, as 'Murder Town'. Hence, it was not unreasonable to conclude that the atmosphere of tension, of agitation, that, at certain times, severely affected the spaces of the building in which the Blaine Company was the only tenant, had its counterpart in the streets of the city outside the building.

More often than not, this city which had once been known as Murder Town was permeated by a yellowish haze. This particular haze was usually so dense that the streetlights of the downtown section as well as the vast, decaying neighborhoods surrounding this area were in operation both day and night. Furthermore, there existed a direct correlation between the murders that took place in the city and the density of the yellowish haze which veiled its streets. Even though no one openly recognized this correspondence, it was a verifiable fact: the heavier this yellowish haze weighed upon the city, the more murders would need to be reported by the local news sources. It was as simple as that.

The actual number of murders could most accurately be traced only in a tabloid newspaper called the *Metro Herald*, which thrived on sensational stories and statistics. The other newspapers, those which purveyed a more dignified image of themselves, proved to be a far less reliable record of both the details of the murders that were occurring throughout the city and also the actual number of these murders. These latter newspapers also failed to indicate any link between the density of the yellowish haze and the city's murder count. True enough, neither did the *Metro Herald* draw direction attention to this link – it was simply a reality that was easier to follow in their pages than in those newspapers with a more dignified image, let alone the radio and television sources, which labored under the burden of delivering their information, respectively, by means of either a human voice or by a human head accompanied by a human voice, lending both of these media a greater immediacy and reality than their printed counterparts. The consequence of the heightened reality of the radio and television news sources was that they could not afford to report anything close to the true quantity or the full details of murders that were always happening. Because if they did offer such reports by means of a human voice, with or without the presence of a human head, they would make themselves intolerable to their listeners and viewers, and ultimately they would lose advertising revenue because their audiences would abandon them, leaving only these human voices and heads reporting one murder after another without anyone listening to them or watching them recite these crimes . . . whereas the newspapers with a dignified image were able to relegate a modicum of such murder stories to the depths of their ample pages, allowing their readers to take or leave these accounts as they wished, while the *Metro Herald* actually thrived upon disseminating such sensational news to a readership eager to consume dispatches on the bleakest, most bizarre, and most scandalous business of the world. Yet even the *Metro Herald* was forced to draw the line at some point when it came to making known to their readers the full quantity as well as the true nature of all of the murderous goings-on in the city to which the Blaine Company had relocated – the city that was once known as Murder Town.

Of course by the time of the company's relocation the epithet of Murder Town was no longer in wide usage, having been eradicated by a sophisticated public relations campaign specifically designed to attract commercial entities like the Blaine Company. Thus, the place formerly known as Murder Town had now acquired an informal civic designation as the Golden City. As anyone might have observed, no specific rationale was ever advanced to justify the city's new persona – the quality of being 'golden' was merely put forth as a given trait, a new identity which was bolstered in the most shameless manner in radio, television, and newspaper ads, not to mention billboards and bro-chures. It was something assumed to be so, as though 'goldenness' – with all the associations attending this term – had always been a vital element of the city. Certainly there was never any reference made, as one might have assumed, to the meteorological phenomenon of the yellowish haze that was truly the preeminent distinction of the physical landscape of the city, including the vast and decaying neighborhoods that surrounded it. In radio, television, and newspaper ads, across billboards, and in the glossy pages of brochures that were mailed out on a worldwide scale, the city was always depicted as a place with clear skies above and tidy metropolitan avenues below. This image, of course, could not have been more at odds with the city's crumbling and all-but-abandoned towers, beneath which were streets so choked with a yellowish haze that one was fortunate to be able to see more than a few yards in any direction.

I knew for a fact that a deal had been struck between the local bureaus of commerce and businesses like the Blaine Company, which could not, for the sake of appearances, relocate their offices to a place whose second name was Murder Town but could easily settle themselves in the Golden City. Nevertheless, it was this place – this haze-choked Murder Town – to which the Blaine Company had been attracted and which well suited, as I well knew, its purposes as a commercial entity.

Not long after the Blaine Company had relocated itself, a memorandum went out to all employees from the office of the founder and president of the company, U G Blaine, a person whom none of us, with the exception of some members of senior management, had ever seen and from whom we had never received a direct communication of any kind, at least not since I had been hired to work in its offices. The memo was brief and simply announced that a 'company-wide restructuring' was imminent, although no dates or details, and no reasoning of any kind, were offered for this dramatic action. Within a few months of the announcement of this obscure 'restructuring', the supervisors of the various departments within the Blaine Company, as well as a few members of upper-level management, were all murdered.

Perhaps I might be allowed a moment to elaborate on the murders I have just mentioned, which were indeed unusual even for a city that had once been known as Murder Town. The most crucial datum which I should impart is that every one of the murders of persons holding management positions at the Blaine Company had taken place within the Golden City on days when the yellowish haze had been especially dense. This fact could have been corroborated by anyone who had taken the least interest in the matter, even if none of the local newspapers (never mind the radio and television reports) ever indicated this connection. Nonetheless, it was quite conspicuous, if one only took the time to glance out the window on certain days when the streets outside were particularly hazy or particularly yellowish, what was in the works. Sometimes I would peek over the enclosure that surrounded my desk and look out into the streets thick with haze. On those occasions I would think to myself, 'Another one of them will be murdered today.' And without exception this would be the case: before the day was out, or sometime during the night, the body of another supervisor, and sometimes a member of upper-level management, would be found lying dead somewhere in the Golden City.

Most often the murders took place as the victims were walking from their cars on their way into work or walking back to their cars after the workday was over, while some of the crimes transpired when the victims were actually inside their cars. Less frequently was the body of a supervisor, or someone of even higher rank within the company, found dead in the evening hours or on weekends. The reason that far fewer of these murders occurred during the evening and on weekends was blatant, even if no one ever made an issue of it. As I have already pointed out, these murders always took place in the Golden City, and even needed to take place there. However, very few of the supervisors, and certainly none of the members of upper-level management, resided within the city limits for the simple reason that they could afford to live in one of the outlying suburbs, where the yellowish haze was seldom as dense and quite often not even visible, or at least not visible to the unaided or unobservant eye. Consequently the victims had scant motivation to make an appearance in the Golden City after working hours or on weekends, for there was nothing, or very little, to attract anyone to this place – and many things that gave cause to avoid it – other than that this happened to be the location where one was forced to come to work. Yet these persons, who spent as little time as possible in the Golden City, were exclusively the ones, out of the large roster of those employed by the Blaine Company, to be viciously murdered there. Or so it was in the beginning.

On some days more than one supervisor's body would be discovered exhibiting the signs of the most violent physical attack, which often suggested the work of more than one assailant, although the crime scene otherwise suggested no evidence of a premeditated conspiracy or thoughtful planning. They all seemed, in fact, to be makeshift affairs.

Sometimes they were crude assaults with whatever objects might have been close at hand (such as a fragment of crumbling sidewalk or a piece of broken window in a back alley). Often the cause of death was simply strangulation or even suffocation in which lice-ridden rags had been jammed deep into the victim's throat. Quite often it was just a beating unto death that left indications of more than one pair of pummeling fists and more than one kind of savagely kicking shoe. Frequently the corpses of these unfortunate supervisors, and the occasional member of upper-level management, were stripped of their clothing, as well as robbed of their money and other valuable effects. This was typical of so many of the murders in the Golden City, a fact that could be verified by the many detectives who interviewed almost everyone at the Blaine Company in the course of their investigations of these crimes, which, in the absence of any other peculiar facts of evidence, were attributed to the numerous derelicts who made their home in the city's streets.

There was, of course, the salient fact – which did not escape the investigating detectives but which, for some reason, they never saw as a relevant issue – that for quite some time all of the victims who worked at the Blaine Company offices had attained the level of supervisor, if not an even higher position in the company. I doubt that the detectives were even aware that it was in the nature of a supervisor's function at the company to foment exactly the kind of violent and even murderous sentiments that would lead low-level staff to form images in their minds of doing away with these people, however we tried to cast such imagined scenes from our minds as soon as they began to form. And now that all of these supervisors had been murdered, we only had each other upon whom to exercise our violent thoughts and fantasies. This situation was aggravated by the tension that derived from our concern over the likely installation of an entirely new group of supervisors throughout the company.

As most of the lower staff employees realized, it was possible to become accustomed to the violent thoughts and fantasies inspired by a supervisor of long standing, and for precisely this reason these supervisors would often be replaced in their position because they were no longer capable of inspiring fresh images of violence in the minds of those they were charged with supervising. With the arrival of a newly appointed supervisor there was inevitably a revival of just the sort of tension that developed into an office atmosphere in which you could barely see a few feet in any direction whenever you were required to move about the aisleways and hallways of the building to which the company had relocated not long before these events which I have chosen to document transpired. It was therefore welcome news to employees when it was made known, by means of a brief memo from one of the highest members of senior management, that none of the murdered supervisors would be replaced and that this position was to be permanently eliminated as part of the scheme for restructuring the company.

The relief experienced among the lower staff of the various departments and divisions of the Blaine Company that they would not have to face the prospect of newly appointed supervisors – or supervisors of any kind, since they had all been murdered – allowed the tension which had been so severe and pervasive to abate, thereby clearing the air around the offices from its previous condition of a blurry atmosphere of agitation and also clearing our minds of the violent thoughts and fantasies that we had come to direct so viciously at one another. However, this state of relative well-being was only temporary and was soon replaced by symptoms of acute apprehension and anxiety. This reversal occurred following a company-wide meeting held in the sub-basement of the building where the Blaine offices had been relocated.

While the senior officers who called for this meeting readily admitted that a sub-basement in an old and crumbling office building was perhaps not the ideal place to hold a company-wide meeting, it was nevertheless the only space large enough to accommodate the company's full staff of employees and was thought preferable to convening at a site elsewhere in the Golden City, since we would then be required to travel through the yellowish haze which lately had become far more consistently dense owing to 'seasonal factors', according to the radio and television reports of local meteorologists. Thus we all came to be huddled in the dim and dirty realm of the building's sub-basement, where we were required to stand for lack of adequate seating and where the senior officers of the company addressed us from a crude platform constructed of thin wooden planks which creaked and moaned throughout this session of speeches and announcements, their words sounding throughout that sub-basement space as hollow and dreamlike echoes.

What we were told, in essence, was that the Blaine Company was positioning itself to become a 'dominant presence in the world marketplace', in the rather vague words of an executive vice president. This declaration struck nearly everyone who stood crushed together in that sub-basement as a preposterous ambition, given that the company provided no major products or services to speak of, its principal commercial activity consisting almost wholly of what I would describe as *manipulating documents* of one sort or another, none of which had any great import or interest beyond a narrow and financially marginal base of customers, including such clients as a regional chain of dry cleaners, several far-flung restaurants that served inex- pensive or at most moderately priced fare, some second-rate facilities featuring dog races that were in operation only part of a given year, and a few private individuals whose personal affairs were such that they required – or perhaps only persuaded themselves out of vanity that they required – the type of document manipulation in which the Blaine Company almost exclusively specialized. However, it was soon revealed to us that the company had plans to become active in areas far beyond, and quite different from, its former specialization in manipulating documents. This announcement was delivered by an elderly man who was introduced to us as Henry Winston, the new Vice President of Development. Mr Winston spoke in a somewhat robotic tone as he recited to us the radical transformations the company would need to undergo in order to make, or remake, itself into a dominant force in the world market-place, although he never disclosed the full nature that these transformations, or 'restructurings', as they were called, would take. Nor did Mr Winston specify the new areas of commercial activity in which the company would be engaged in the very near future.

During the course of Mr Winston's address, none of us could help noticing that he seemed terribly out of place among the other members of senior management who occupied that rickety wooden platform constructed es-pecially for this meeting. His suit appeared to have been tailored for a larger body than the bony frame that now shifted beneath the high-priced materials which hung upon the old man. And his thick white hair was heavily greased and slicked back, yet as he spoke it began to sprout up in places, as if his lengthy, and in some places yellowed locks were not accustomed to the grooming now forced upon them.

As murmurs began to arise among those of us pressed together in that dim and dirty sub-basement, Mr Winston's mechanical monologue was cut short by one of the other senior officers, who took the spotlight from the old man and proceeded to deliver the final announcement of the meeting. Yet even before this final announcement was made by a severe-looking woman with close-cropped hair, many of those among the crowd huddled into the confines of that sub-basement had already guessed or intuited its message. From the moment we descended into that lowest level of the building by way of the freight elevator, there was a feeling expressed by several employees that an indefinable presence inhabited that place, something that was observing us very closely without ever presenting a lucid image of itself. Several people from the lower staff even claimed to have glimpsed a peculiar figure in the dark reaches of the sub-basement, a shape of some kind that seemed to maneuver about the edges of the congregation, a hazy human outline that drifted as slowly and silently as the yellowish haze in the streets of the Golden City and was seen to be of a similar hue.

So by the time the woman with the close-cropped hair made what might otherwise have been a striking revelation, most of the lower staff were beyond the point of receiving the news as any great surprise. 'Therefore,' continued the severe-looking woman, 'the role of those supervisors who have been so tragically lost to our organization will now be taken over by none other than the founder and president of the Blaine Company – Mr U G Blaine. In an effort to facilitate the restructuring of our activities as a business, Mr Blaine will henceforth be taking a *direct hand* in every aspect of the company's day-to-day functions. Unfortunately, Mr Blaine could not be present today, but he extends his assurance that he looks forward to working with each and every one of you in the near future. So, if there are no questions' – and there were none – 'this meeting is therefore concluded.' And as we ascended in the freight elevator to return to our desks, nothing at all was said about the plans revealed to us for the company's future.

Later that day, however, I heard the voices of some of my coworkers in conversation nearby the enclosure that surrounded my desk. 'It's perfectly insane what they're doing,' whispered a woman whose voice I recognized as that of a longtime employee and a highly productive manipulator of documents. Others in this group more or less agreed with this woman's evaluation of the company's grandiose ambition of becoming a dominant force in the world marketplace. Finally someone said, 'I'm thinking of giving my notice. For some time now I've been regretting that I ever followed the company to this filthy city.' The person who spoke these words was someone known around the office as The Bow Tie Man, a name granted to him due to his penchant for sporting this eponymous item of apparel on a daily basis. He seemed to enjoy the distinction he gained by wearing a wide variety of bow ties rather than ordinary straight ties, or even no tie at all. Although there were possibly millions of men around the world who also wore bow ties as a signature of sartorial distinction, he was the only one in the Blaine Company offices to do so. This practice of his allowed him to express a mode of personal identity, however trivial and illusory, as if such a thing could be achieved merely by adorning oneself with a particular item of apparel or even by displaying particular character traits such as a reserved manner or a high degree of intelligence, all and any of which qualities were shared by millions and millions of persons past and present and would continue to be exhibited by millions and millions of persons in the future, making the effort to perpetrate a distinctive sense of an identity apart from other persons or creatures, or even inanimate objects, no more than a ludicrous charade.

It was after I heard The Bow Tie Man proclaim that he was of a mind to 'give his notice' that I stepped away from my desk and walked over to join the conversation being carried on by some of my coworkers. 'And after you give your notice,' I asked The Bow Tie Man, 'then what? Where will you go? What other place could you find that would be any different?' Then the woman whose voice I had previously recognized as that of a longtime member of the company's staff spoke up, protesting that it was absolutely deranged for the company to imagine that it could ever become a dominant force in the world marketplace. 'Do you really think so?' I replied. 'Haven't you observed that there is a natural tendency, deranged or not, for all such entities as the Blaine Company, for any kind of business or government or even private individual, to extend themselves as far as possible – to force themselves on the world as much as they can, either by becoming a dominant commercial entity or merely by wearing bow ties every day, thereby imposing themselves on the persons and things around them, imposing what they are or what they believe themselves to be without regard or respect for anything else aside from how far they can reach out into the world and put their seal upon it, even stretching out into other worlds, shouting commands at the stars themselves and claiming the universe as their own?'

By that point, I think my coworkers were taken aback, not as much by the words I had spoken as by the fact that I had spoken to them at all, something I had never done apart from the verbal exchanges required by our work as document manipulators. From their expressions I could see that my speaking to them in this way was somehow monstrous and wrong – a freak happening whose occurrence signified something they did not wish to name. Almost immediately afterward the group broke up, and we all returned to our desks.

That afternoon the yellowish haze of the Golden City was especially dense and pushed itself heavily against the windows of the building where the Blaine Company had relocated itself. And on the very same day that upper-level management had announced to us that none of the murdered supervisors would be replaced and that U G Blaine himself was going to take a direct hand in the day-to-day operations of each department and division within the company, it seemed that his supervisory presence was already among us.

The most conspicuous early sign of what I will call the 'Blaine presence' was the distinct yellowish tint which now permeated the company's office space. Less obvious was the sense, which a number of persons had previously experienced during the company-wide meeting, that we were at all times under the eye of something we could not see but which was intimately aware of our every word and action.

Before the day was over, everyone in the office seemed to have gained a silent understanding of why we had relocated to the Golden City and why this place, which had once been known as Murder Town, was so well suited to the purposes of commercial entities like the Blaine Company ... or was at least perceived to be so by the heads of such corporate bodies.

By the following business day there was no longer any talk around the office about the deranged strategy of the company to become a dominant force in the world market-place. And no one commented on the absence of the man who wore bow ties each and every day. Perhaps the others actually believed that he had given his notice – a course of action he had suggested he might take – even though none of his personal items had been removed from his desk. Since the supervisor of our department had been murdered like all the others, there was no one whose duty it was to be concerned with the failure of The Bow Tie Man to show up at the office, just as there was no one who proffered any information about the meaning of his absence. After a few days had passed, his desk was occupied by a new employee, a man whom no one had ever seen working elsewhere in the company and who did not seem like the sort of person any company would hire to manipulate documents. His age was difficult to discern because his face was almost entirely obscured by shaggy strands of unwashed hair and an ample growth of untended beard, both of which were streaked with the discoloration which we noticed affected anything that was subject to longtime exposure to the peculiar atmospheric elements of the Golden City. As for the clothes worn by our new coworker, they appeared to be very much in the same style as his predecessor who formerly inhabited that particular desk. However, due to the length of the new employee's beard, it was not possible to verify whether or not he was wearing a bow tie each and every day. And no one in the office desired to look close enough to find out if this was the case. Nevertheless, there was one woman whom I overheard telling another that she was going to check on The Bow Tie Man in order to establish what had become of him. Then she herself failed to show up for work the next day. Afterward no one else pursued the disappearance of either of these two employees, nor that of any of several other employees who on a fairly regular basis now began to drop out of the ranks of the lower staff at the Blaine Company, which by this time was known to the world simply as 'Blaine'.

Needless to say, the degree of tension that now pervaded the offices at Blaine was once again at an extremely high level. Yet this tense environment, which had always served as a hothouse for the most violent thoughts and fantasies among company personnel, no longer had an effect on the atmosphere of our workplace, such that you could not see more than a few feet in front of your face. Instead, the office space continued to be evenly permeated by a yellowish tint. While I have already identified this distinct yellowish coloration of the office atmosphere with what I have called the Blaine presence, others around me – and throughout the company – held the view that the haze which choked the streets of the Golden City had somehow seeped into the building where we spent each day manipulating documents. But it seemed to me that these differing explanations were in fact complementary. In my view there was a terrible equation between the Blaine presence, which now supervised every activity throughout the company, even the smallest manipulations of the most insignificant documents, and the yellowish haze casting itself so densely over the Golden City – a place that seemed so well suited to the purposes of commercial entities like Blaine, which of course were merely extensions of the purposes of human entities like U G Blaine himself, specifically his seemingly preposterous ambition to turn his business into a dominant force in the world marketplace. All of this remained hypothetical for some time . . . until one day a certain turn of events allowed me to confirm my suspicions and at the same time – after so much patient restraint – enabled me to pursue my own purposes with respect to the relocation of the company.

This turning point came in the form of a summons to the office of the new Vice President of Development, Mr Henry Winston, who was located in a remote part of the building in which Blaine was the only tenant. Mr Winston's office, I noted when I first entered, was a sty. Judging by the stained mattress in a corner behind some rusted filing cabinets and the remnants of food and beverage containers scattered about the floor, Mr Winston had transformed the place into his personal hovel. The Vice President of Development himself was seated behind an old and heavily scarred wooden desk, his arms stretched across the desktop and his head lying sideways upon it in noisy slumber. When I closed the door behind me, Mr Winston slowly awakened and looked up at me, his hair and beard no longer groomed in the way they had been for the sub-basement meeting at which he spoke some months before. And what he had to say to me now still sounded as though he were reading from a script, although the quality of his voice was far less robotic than it had been at the company-wide meeting.

Mr Winston rubbed his eyes and ran his tongue around the inside of his mouth, catching the aftertaste of the sleep I had disturbed. Then, as if he were a busy man, he got right to the point. 'He wants to have a conference with you. There's a . . .' Mr Winston paused a moment, apparently at a loss to recall or properly enunciate his next words. 'A proposal. There's a proposal he has for you . . . a personal proposal.'

Mr Winston then informed me of the time and place for this conference with U G Blaine – after the end of that working day, in a lavatory on one of the uppermost floors of the building. This seemed to be everything that the Vice President of Development was required to communicate to me, and I turned to leave his office. But before I was out the door he blurted out a few words that genuinely seemed to be his own.

'He should never have brought you here,' said Mr Winston, which very well might have been his real name.

'You mean the relocation of the company to this city,' I replied, attempting to clarify the issue.

'That's right. The re-lo-ca-tion,' he said, breaking into a little laugh and revealing an incomplete set of yellow teeth. But he stopped laughing when I looked over my shoulder back at him, focusing my eyes deep into his.

'Mr Blaine isn't entirely responsible,' I said. 'We both know how it is with this city.'

After a brief pause Mr Winston spoke. 'I know you now,' he said as if speaking softly in a dream. 'You were here before . . . when the sky was clear. What did you do?'

I simply smiled at the Vice President of Development and then exited that squalid office, leaving the man inside with his sleep-polluted mouth hanging open in stupefied wonder.

By this juncture in the company's progress, there were no longer many employees remaining who were not of a kind with Henry Winston. One by one all the regular staff stopped appearing for work, and their desks came to be occupied by new persons who always looked like fugitives from the great tribe of derelicts living in the Golden City, a shadow population that moved day and night through that yellowish haze. No doubt they too had made accommodations for themselves in the building, little havens similar to the one I saw in Henry Winston's office. I imagined that such accommodations and a modicum of food may have been offered to them by the company in lieu of a paycheck. This scheme for 'cost-cutting' would alone account for the elevated profits that Blaine had realized in the past quarter. Of course this manner of fiscal growth could not continue much longer, and other measures would need to be taken if the company was truly to become a dominant force in the marketplace of this world or any other. These measures, I assumed, would emerge as the chief topic of the conference U G Blaine had scheduled with me after the close of the working day in a lavatory on one of the uppermost floors of that crumbling building.

When the time came, I began ascending the shaft of stairways – the elevator having ceased to function by that time – in anticipation of my private meeting with the company's president and founder. As I made my way in nearly total darkness up these steps I recalled the day that I came to interview for my position with what was then called the Blaine Company. That interview took place in another building in another city. In the reception area where I waited to be called for my interview there hung a portrait of U G Blaine. It was a flattering-enough likeness of a middle-aged man in a business suit, but the effect of contemplating this portrait was such that I wanted to turn away and purge it from my mind before I started thinking thoughts that I did not want in my head. But I found it impossible to turn away. Fortunately someone came along and called me to my interview before my thoughts reached a pitch of intolerable tension and agitation.

The person who interviewed me asked, among other things, what single personal quality I believed I might possess that would distinguish me for consideration as an employee of the Blaine Company. I hesitated for some time, and even thought it might be best if I gave no reply at all, or a very feeble and conventional response. Instead I spoke some words that I was sure the interviewer wanted to hear and that, in fact, were true. 'My quality,' I said, 'my personal quality is the capacity to drive myself and those around me to the uttermost limits of our potential – to affect persons, and even places, in a way that brings their unsuspected possibilities and purposes out of hiding and into the full light of realization. That is my personal quality.'

As oddly phrased and vehement as this statement might sound to other individuals, it was, I knew, exactly what my interviewer wanted to hear. On the spot I was offered the position for which I had applied at the Blaine Company –

that of a manipulator of documents. When I entered the company's old offices to be interviewed my only purpose was to lose myself in the manipulation of documents, to bury as deeply as I could this passionate personal quality of mine, which had always resulted in the most unfortunate and twisted consequences for those involved, whether it was an individual person or a group of persons or a commercial entity like the Blaine Company. Because my personal quality, as stated to my interviewer at the Blaine Company, was more than a figure of speech or an exaggerated claim for the purposes of self-promotion, even if I have been at a lifelong loss to account for the full force of this extraordinary quality. For years my only purpose had been to suppress this quality, to crush it as best I could. However, after contemplating that portrait of U G Blaine – after seeing written upon that face what I might describe as a 'profoundly baseless sense of purpose in the world' – everything changed inside my head, which I could no longer keep from filling up with strange and violent thoughts and fantasies. 'This company will soon need to relocate,' I thought as I walked away from my interview that day. 'In order to satisfy its sense of purpose as a commercial entity, and the baseless sense of purpose of its founder and president, this company will need to relocate to another place.' And I knew precisely the place that was well suited to the company's purposes . . . and to my own. Thus, when I finally located and entered the small lavatory where U G Blaine wished to confer with me, I was incited to the point of derangement by the grim drama which was now coming to a climax.

'Opportunity awaits you in the Golden City,' I shouted, my voice resounding against the tile walls and floor, the metal doors and porcelain fixtures of the antiquated lavatory surrounding me. 'Opportunity awaits you in the Golden City,' I repeated, mocking the slogan that a public relations company had used to transform the image of the city once known as Murder Town. It was this preposterous dream of changing its public image that made the Golden City ideal for the purposes of Blaine (the company), which held the deranged and preposterous idea that it could ever become a dominant force in the world marketplace, even though its only commercial activity was that of manipulating documents for small-time businesses and a few private individuals. Only in this atmosphere of a crumbling city surrounded by vast, decaying neighborhoods, its streets filled with hordes of wandering derelicts and permeated by a yellowish haze that no meteorologist or scientist of any kind had ever successfully accounted for ... only in this Murder Town could I manage to drive Mr U G Blaine to the uttermost limit of his potential – just as I had driven this city itself, whose streets I inhabited for a time, to the vile and devious limit of its potential, leaving behind an inexplicable yellowish haze, a mere side effect of the things that I had done there, things that I was born to do as a freak of this world (or perhaps another world altogether, so unknown am I to myself), things that my freakish nature learned to do over many years, and things that made me seek my own burial in an occupation where I could forget my freakish self and everything I knew about this world where I did not belong. Only here could Blaine be made to realize his unsuspected possibilities and purposes, especially that baseless sense of purpose which I could not escape seeing in that portrait of a middle-aged man in a business suit.

Of course it was not a man in a business suit who awaited my arrival in that small lavatory – it was the Blaine presence, as I called it, that pervaded the bright little room with its yellow tint. 'Your restructuring of the company has been a great success,' I said to the Blaine presence, which now quivered and curled about the room in trembling, yellow-tinted waves. 'Soon it will be just you and your derelicts in this building. You will be the dominant force in the marketplace of the Golden City, manipulating all the documents in town. But you will never go further than that. This is where you belong. This is where you will stay. And there's nothing either of us can do to change that. You think that I can assist you in extending your power and influence, your marketplace dominance, but I came to tell you that no such thing will ever happen. This place is your uttermost limit.'

The Blaine presence was now becoming extremely agitated, its yellow tint swirling about the room and batting itself against the walls. 'There's no use in blaming me for what you are,' I screamed. 'You're the creator of a marketplace for violent thoughts and fantasies. I saw that in the portrait of the middle-aged man in a business suit, and I can feel it in the presence you have now made of yourself. That's all there can ever be for you in this world.'

At that point I picked up a wastepaper container that stood by the lavatory sink and was shaped like a bullet with a rounded point. Across the room was a small window with panes of frosted glass. I smashed those glass panes by ramming the rounded top of the wastepaper container into it with all the violent force within me. Through the smashed panes of that window in a lavatory on one of the uppermost floors of the building you could see out over the city, the moon shining down through the yellowish haze. 'There,' I shouted while pointing out the broken window. 'Go out into your world of haze. That's your element now. And you can't survive beyond its limits. The limits of the Golden City.'

I felt a powerful, almost cyclonic gust sweep past me on all sides, even moving through me as it soared out the broken window and blended into the yellowish haze beyond, leaving behind it a room charged with the residue of vicious and violent impulses.

After that night, the Golden City was rechristened as Murder Town. Early the next morning, the streetlights still shining through the yellowish haze, brutally mauled bodies were discovered lying in every street of the city and far into the vast, decaying neighborhoods surrounding it. For a time news reports broadcasted by radio and television and printed in newspapers with a dignified image as well as tabloid rags like the *Metro Herald* – where I once worked as a reporter myself – were concerned with nothing but these murders, which they called 'Murders of Mystery' or 'Mysterious Mass Murders'.

However, it was not long before serious consideration was given to the possibility that these were not murders at all but the consequences of what the *Metro Herald* designated the 'Yellow Plague', because the bodies of the victims all displayed jaundiced blotches that overworked hospital personnel, police investigators, and morgue attendants had at first assumed to be bruises caused by violent attacks. For a day or so city officials had the opportunity to present the cause of these astonishingly lurid and numerous deaths as, quite possibly, an instance of a mysterious disease rather than of mysterious murder. With the cooperation of local law enforcement and medical officials, along with the services of a sophisticated public relations campaign, the issue of how such an incredible number of corpses might have been produced during a single night could have been confused long enough for the city to waver between its old reputation as a place of murder and an entirely new identity as a place of disease. Of course, given the alternative of henceforth being known to the world as the 'City of the Yellow Plague', on the one hand, or as 'Murder Town', on the other, the latter appellative seemed the preferable choice.

Apparently unrelated to the Mystery Murders, according to news reports disseminated by all the local media, was the discovery of the body of a middle-aged man dressed in a worn business suit in a suburb just outside the city limits. Eventually identified as U G Blaine, the corpse was found lying in the parking lot of a small outdoor shopping center. Investigators uncovered no signs that might have connected Blaine's death to those which took place the night before in Murder Town. To all appearances the man had simply collapsed and died in a place where the yellowish haze of what was once known as the Golden City dissolved altogether, giving way to the lucid atmosphere of an upper-class suburb contiguous with the city's outlying neighborhoods.

On that same morning that Blaine's body was found, I walked through the deserted streets of a city where others were still afraid to walk, strolling calmly through the stillness and the yellowish haze. For a moment I felt that I had finally driven myself to my limit, and I was content as errant pages from local newspapers flapped idiotically along the sidewalk and streetlights glared down upon me.

But before the morning had passed I was ready to move on – to relocate once more. My purpose, for a time, had exhausted itself. But now I could see there were other cities, other people and places. I could see all the world as if it loomed only a few feet in front of me – its every aspect so clear to my eyes that I would never be able to drive it from my mind until the last of my violent thoughts and fantasies had been fulfilled. Even though I knew in the depths of myself that it was all just another preposterous ambition, a false front propped up by baseless purposes and dreams, I could not help thinking to myself – 'I have a special plan for this world.'

May this document, unmanipulated, stand as my declaration of purpose.

THE NIGHTMARE NETWORK

CLASSIFIED AD I

A multinational corporation is dreaming. We are an organization of more than 100 thousand souls (full-time) and are presently seeking individuals willing to trade their personal lot for a share in our dream. Entry-level positions are now available for self-possessed persons who can see beyond the bottom line to a bottomless realm of possibilities. Our enterprise is now thriving in a tough, global marketplace and has taken on a life all its own. If you are a committed, focused individual with a hunger to be part of something far greater than yourself . . . our door is now open. Your life need not be a nightmare of failure and resentment. Join us. Outstanding benefits.

An opening scene

Dawn in the rain forest. Sunlight begins flickering through the green luxuriance and appears here and there as radiant pools upon the soft, dark earth. A tribe of hunter-gatherers lies sleeping near a shallow stream. The camera pans from one inanely tranquil face to another. Thus far no noises of any kind occur on the soundtrack – no rustling in the underbrush, no burbling of the shallow stream, no screeching from the rain forest's animal life. While surveying the sleeping tribe, the camera moves in for a close-up of one hunter whose face is anything but inanely tranquil. It is not even the face of one who lives in the rain forest. Although the man is practically naked, and a sharpened stick is lying within reach of his sleeping form, his skin is pale and his hair neatly styled. Now his features are becoming contorted, as if he is experiencing a nightmare. He seems to be talking in his sleep, but thus far there are no noises of any kind on the soundtrack. Finally the silence is broken by the spasmic drone of an alarm clock. The eyes of the hunter suddenly open and stare in panic; his pale skin is running with sweat. The alarm clock continues to sound.

Orientation video

A pretty, dark-haired actress in a business suit is standing amid a maze of desks, talking to the camera and expertly gesturing. The occupants of the desks are seemingly oblivious to her presence. At the end of the video the actress smartly crosses her arms over her chest, fixes a stern expression on her face, and utters the corporate motto which introduced the video as a title ('Think Again'). As she continues to stare into the camera the scene around her begins to change: shadows drift about the maze of desks and the faces of all the employees become rotten and corroded, as if they are being afflicted with leprosy in fast motion. One by one they rise from behind their desks and succumb to the strange fidgety conniptions of a *danse macabre*. Under the stress of these fitful, brittle movements their limbs break off and fall to the floor, where the shadows move in to devour them. Noses and ears quickly wither, lips peel back to reveal broken teeth, eyeballs shrivel in their sockets. The pretty, dark-haired actress continues to stare into the camera with a stern expression.

Memo from the CEO

As the forces operating in today's marketplace become more shadowy and incomprehensible we must recommit ourselves every second of every day to a ceaseless striving for that elusive dream which we all share and which none of us can remember, if it ever existed in the first place. And if anyone thinks that, as all the world races toward the same elusive dream, our competition isn't fully prepared to gnaw off its own genitals to get to the promised land before us and keep it for themselves . . . think again.

From a supervisor's notebook

. . . And if I were determined to live solely on the flesh of my own staff, with no access to the staffs of other surviving supervisors or any other personnel, the greatest challenge to present itself would be maintaining each of them in an edible state, while also regulating my consumption of these bodies. Perhaps I should try to keep them alive; in that case I could simply restrict myself to ingesting only those elements capable of regeneration, such as blood. Even so, I do dream about their armpits and elbows . . . those of the men as well as the women. I think that during this time of cannibalistic survival I would particularly savor the more wrinkly parts of the human anatomy.

The hunter

The green doors of an elevator slide open, revealing a man in a dark business suit. He is standing dead center in the framing shot, and his hair is noticeably neat and well styled. In his right hand is an automatic pistol with a nickel-plated handle. He holds the weapon close to his side as he steps out of the elevator and begins walking swiftly down one brightly lit hallway after another. A series of offices with open doors passes on either side of him. At the end of one of the hallways he stops before a door that is closed. He removes a security card from the inside pocket of his suit and pushes it into the thin slot beside the door. There is a soft, droning sound as the man opens the door and walks inside, leaving his security card behind. Beyond the door he moves into a maze of desks, at each of which a man or a woman is seated. The man stops at the center of the maze, which now seems to spin around him like a carousel. Cacophonous music in waltz time begins rising on the soundtrack, becoming louder and faster as it approaches a painful crescendo. The music is then cut off by the sudden report of a single gunshot. The room stops spinning. The man lies dead within the maze of desks, his shattered skull pouring blood upon the floor. Later the coworkers of this man disclose that for some time he had complained about hearing barely audible messages on his telephone every time he made or received a call in the office. Officers of the company merely shake their heads in condescending sympathy. The following day they authorize financing for the installation of a new telephone system.

CLASSIFIED AD II

Major Supercorp in the process of expanding its properties and market-base has limited openings for Approved Labor in domestic and off-shore sites (real and virtual). We are among the biggest legitimate multi-monopolies on the world scene and our Corporate Persona is one that any AL can adopt in good conscience. Experience in sensory-deprived conditions preferred. Knowledge of outlawed dialects on the Nightmare Network a plus. Standard survival package of benefits. Prehistoric ALs okay with biologic documentation from transport agency.

The farmers

An unplanted field beneath a gray prehistoric sky. The camera slowly pans from left to right, revealing several figures at various positions in the foreground and background. Each of them is wearily gouging the earth with crude implements typical of the incipient age of agriculture. They are clothed in tunics made from animal hides which are tattered and filthy. Their long hair and weasely beards are matted and lice-ridden. The camera pauses for a long-shot of farmers and field to reinforce the profound tedium of this panorama of a Stone Age planting season. Almost simultaneously the figures all freeze and then look up from the earth upon which their eyes have been previously fixed. What they have seen is the greenish, glowing dome that now hovers over the field and has closed off its perimeter. Some of the farmers begin running about in panic-stricken hysterics, while the rest fall to the ground unconscious or dead from the shock of the inexplicable phenomenon which, given their quasi-feral instincts, they perceive as an overpowering menace. Shafts of greenish light begin to shoot out from various points of the dome, seizing upon each of the farmers and levitating them high above the field. Even the dead bodies are captured and carried beyond the inner surface of the dome. The field now stands empty, the primitive farming tools lie abandoned on the ground. Superimposed on this scene the following legend appears:

THE NIGHTMARE OF THE PAST
BECOMES THE DREAM OF THE FUTURE.
ONEIRICON: ONE WORLD, ONE DREAM

On the nightmare network

Our names are unknown and our faces are shadows drifting across an infinite blackness. Our voices have been stifled to a soft murmur in a madman's ear. We are the proud failures with only a single joy left to us – to inflict rampant damage on those who have fed themselves on our dreams and to choke ourselves on our own nightmares. In sum, we are expediters of the apocalypse. There is nothing left to save, if there ever was anything . . . if there ever could be. All we desire (in all our bitterness) is to go to our ruin *in our own way* – with a little style and a lot of noise.

The harvest

The main grid at Security Central indicates that there is a crisis situation in sub-cube six-o-six, which is located several hundred kilometers below ground level. A minor security officer explains to his supervisor that, for an undetermined period of time, the Nightmare Network has been engaged in undetected communication with all one hundred and fifty of the ALs in six-o-six, feeding them images and data on their computer screens. A hasty check of all monitors reveals that personnel in that particular sub-cube have been in a malignant dream state for at least seventy-two hours. Signals to the monitors have been altered so that visual and auditory data from sub-cube seven-o-seven were substituted for those that were supposed to emanate from six-o-six. The system was not programmed to indicate an alert after detecting the duplication of data, an oversight that would be corrected in the future. In the present, a heavily armed security force descends to six-o-six for the purpose of assessment and possible remedial action. What they discover there causes some of the new recruits to vomit into the face masks attached to their helmets. The entire cube is in an uproar, and there are mutilated bodies everywhere. The ALs who are still alive are running amok within a maze of computer terminals. Most of them are naked and covered in blood; some have adorned themselves with entrails that dangle around their necks or have wrapped flayed skin about their heads. Many of them are eating the flesh of the dead and the dying. An influx of blood and other bodily fluids has caused short-circuits in many of the computers, which are spraying sparks and occasionally electrocute one of the dervishing ALs. The computers that are still in working order have the same message upon their screens. In flashing, luminous letters all of them read: GREETINGS FROM THE NIGHTMARE NETWORK.

CLASSIFIED AD III

OneiriCon requires Employment Units with autonomous or semi-autonomous programming to oversee a workforce of Nonconscious ALs. Some contact with Noncons or their semblances may be involved (visual desensitization or nihilization for all EUs paid for by OneiriCon). Remember: there are no bad dreams if there is only one dream; there can be no outlaws where there is only one law. Artificial entities from the Nightmare Network that attempt to impersonate Employment Units will be discovered and reprogrammed to exist in an eternal state of hallucinated agony. Imperfectly functioning EUs will be discovered and mercifully deleted. Possible elevation to part- or full-time status as cyberpersonage (with commensurate benefits and restrictions) for all qualified units.

Masters and slaves

Twilight in an ancient desert land. The slaves have all been gathered before an enormous, semi-circular platform. Behind the platform the spires and towers of the great palace are outlined against a fading sky. Before the platform is a sea of loin-clothed slaves kneeling in the desert sand, which has grown cool with the setting of the sun. The camera focuses on the central part of the platform, where a number of slaves have been tied to a row of freestanding pillars.

From the crown of each pillar emanates a clean, steady flame that provides generous illumination for the entire platform and places special emphasis on the restrained bodies of the slaves. On either side of the platform are the seated figures of the royal family, priests and high-priests, high-ranking military officers, and other notable persons of the kingdom. After the sun has disappeared behind some distant sand dunes, leaving tens of thousands of slaves in total darkness, the proceedings finally commence. The head executioner and several of his assistants now ascend the enormous platform from a stairway to the right. The camera follows behind them as they approach the flaming pillars where the bound slaves await an elaborate regimen of torture that will continue throughout the night and end with their simultaneous deaths at sunrise. But when the head executioner reaches the center of the platform and turns to receive a sinister-looking instrument held out to him by one of his assistants, he suddenly freezes in position – a statue with outstretched arms and open hands. At this point, one of the slaves kneeling toward the front of the massive audience rises to his feet and jumps onto the platform. No one makes a move to stop him. The slave walks up to the flaming pillars and scans the horrified faces of his fellows who are anticipating a night of agony and, ultimately, death. After a while he simply shrugs and turns away from them. Stepping over to the head executioner, the slave looks the frozen figure up and down. With the fingers of his right hand he probes beneath the wide gold neckband which the head executioner is wearing and which is symbolic of his office. Some moments pass with no change in the gruesome functionary's state. The slave now appears to be slightly exasperated. He removes his fingers from the gold neckband, and with the heel of his right hand gives the statue-like figure a sharp rap on the side of the head. The head executioner then goes into motion once again, seizing the proffered implement of pain and picking up where he left off. Before returning to his place, the slave glances around, as if to see if any of the others might require maintenance, excepting those tied to the flaming pillars, who are the only living persons among the assemblage of automatons occupying the platform. He then rejoins his fellow slaves, none of whom in any way acknowledge that he was ever absent from their ranks, although they too are all flesh-and-blood beings. Briefly deferred, the long night of torture and death can finally begin – followed by a feast upon the bodies of the dead.

Within the system

Having absorbed or destroyed every one of its competitors, OneiriCon begins to deteriorate. It is then that its Governing Executives conspire to create a number of puppet entities which would provide a degree of competition for the organization, thus reinfusing its lower-level executives and other conflict-driven personnel with a sense of purpose and staving off total degeneration. (The majority of OneiriCon's employees – the billions of ALs and even greater numbers of EUs – have existed in a benign dream state for so long that they seem to require no external stimuli of any kind, although this remains a matter of debate among the organization's scientists, who are highly adept at providing themselves with trumped-up mysteries and challenges.) For a time Project Puppetcorps succeeds admirably, and some of the artificial corporate entities do quite well in the market-place, or what is left of it. In the end, however, they too are absorbed or destroyed by OneiriCon. Unable to reconcile themselves to the prospect of terminal stagnancy for an organization that has always subsisted on the principle of ceaseless growth, many of the Governing Executives voluntarily submit to devolutionary brain surgery and afterward join the ranks of Noncon ALs. Others have themselves transported to the distant past, where they become slaves of a society governed by automatons, thus affording their competitive spirits new objects of resistance and a low point of orientation from which they can once again work their way to the top. The remaining GEs occupy their time by playing extravagant and intensely cruel practical jokes on one another. In this manner most of them are killed off or so severely damaged that they can no longer function at any level of the organization. Then all of a sudden a solution seems to present itself to one of the highest-ranking GEs, who is an old-timer recovering from a major substitution procedure in his own private medical cell. At some stage of his convalescence the ancient exec is made to regain consciousness of himself and his surroundings, a situation that is not supposed to occur during the normal course of these procedures. When he becomes fully awake he is surprised, and somewhat horrified, to find that grafted to his torso is the decapitated head of a corporeal Noncon. This state of affairs seems to him to exceed even the wildest of the pranks lately being perpetrated at OneiriCon. The head of the Noncon does not appear to be alive, so the old man is startled when its mouth pops open and begins to emit a long thin strip of paper much like those produced by ticker-tape machines that reported stock values during the twentieth century. With a sense of atavistic nostalgia, the GE picks up the tape and reads the words printed upon it. The words are these: 'How about letting the Nightmare Network have some fun?' Possessing the innovative vision and cunning genius of administrative life-forms through the ages, the old Governing Executive exclaims: 'We are saved!' Then he dies, his body succumbing to the trauma incurred by its assimilation of the Noncon's foreign tissue. Fortunately a video record of the entire incident is preserved.

The dreams of a double agent

There is considerable resistance at OneiriCon to the proposal that the organization join forces with the Nightmare Network. None of the surviving GEs denies that the concept of a *hostile merger* with one's own anti-entity, corporately speaking, is a risky venture. On the other hand, admitting such a parasite into their system for the strict purpose of revitalizing aggressive impulses – an inoculation, as it were – seems the only alternative to the progressive atrophy and ultimate shut-down with which the organization will otherwise be faced. It is therefore agreed (at the highest level) that all personnel at OneiriCon (of every level and status of reality and consciousness) will also be in the employ of the Nightmare Network. This initiative will in effect make everyone in both camps of these long-conflicting entities into a double agent. In a telepathic memo, one of the most powerful GEs warns his peers: 'Obviously there can be no official sanction at OneiriCon of our so-called merger with the Nightmare Network, since the sole purpose of this arrangement is that of a motivational strategy for our employees, both real and virtual. This organization certainly has no intention of becoming mother hog for an over-populated system of deadbeat operatives (as well as their semblances) who are drawing an easy paycheck for every gesture of either espionage or counter-espionage, every act of sabotage or anti-sabotage, whether they try to pass counterfeit data through the OneiriCon circuits or inform on their own semblances for attempting same.' In other words, no single agent in either camp must ever be made aware that their personal betrayal is merely part of a large-scale, cooperative venture between two age-old enemies. Otherwise, the potential abuses and slacking off on both sides might undermine the whole arrangement. Thus, infiltration of OneiriCon by the Nightmare Network, *and vice versa*, has to be pursued simultaneously, taking place in a most surreptitious manner, one recruit at a time, until there is a perfect similitude between the two entities. This process is swiftly completed throughout the Nightmare Network, where individual and collective values tend toward subversion without regard for rational pretexts. All of them being natural-born losers and self-destructive organisms of the worst sort, they run crotch-first into the bargain, some even adopting multiple identities so that they can experience more than once the monstrous thrill of selling out their own futile aspirations. The camera pans a crowd of faces whose eyes are bleary with sedition and a lust for all-out pandemonium. To no one's surprise, the response of the personnel at OneiriCon is identical to that of their counterparts at the Nightmare Network. Subsequently there ensues an epoch of complex, proliferating intrigues and conspiracies among the ranks of double agents, whose agendas become so densely intertwined that they are virtually indistinguishable. Even the Governing Executives of OneiriCon, many of whom are defectors from the Nightmare Network, throw themselves into the depths of the new order and lose all sense of identity in the ever-expanding nebula of blind ambition, which possesses a power and impetus that belongs entirely to itself. After a time no one can be sure whom they are serving whenever they commit any given act of either sabotage or support. There are no longer two distinct entities in well-defined opposition; there is only a great chaos of confused purposes churning in darkness. Each entity is disappearing into the maw of the other, thereby realizing their most cherished dreams and worst nightmares of oblivion. At last, it seems, they will have managed to close the whole thing down.

CLASSIFIED DISTRESS SIGNAL

Vast organization of delirious images and impulses seeking Sustenance Input for its decaying systems. All data considered, including polluted discharges from the old Nightmare Network and after-images of degenerated EUs and ALs (Con, Noncon, or OneiriCon). Total atrophy and occlusion of all circuits imminent – next stop, the Nowhere Network. Your surplus information – shadows and semblances lying dormant in long-unaccessed files – could be used to replenish our hungry database. No image too hideous; no impulse too attenuated or corrupt. Our organization has a life of its own, but without the continuous input of cheap data we cannot compete in today's apocalyptic marketplace. From a rotting mutation, great illusions may grow. Don't let us go belly up while the black empty spaces of the galaxy reverberate with hellish laughter. A multi-dimensional, semi-organic discorporation is dreaming . . .

The signal repeats, steadily deteriorating, and then fades into nothingness. Long shot of the universe. There is no one behind the camera.

TEATRO GROTTESCO

by Thomas Ligotti

In this peerless collection of dark fictions, Ligotti follows the literary tradition that began with Edgar Allan Poe: portraying characters that are outside of anything that might be called normal life, depicting strange locales far off the beaten track, and rendering a grim vision of human existence as a perpetual nightmare. Just by entering his unique world where odd little towns and dark sectors are peopled with clowns and hideous puppets, and where tormented individuals and blackly comical eccentrics play out their doom, is to risk your own vision of the world.

9780753513743